国家出版基金项目
NATIONAL PUBLICATION FOUNDATION

# 梅葛

云南省民族民间文学楚雄调查队　搜集翻译整理

邓之宇　张立玉　英译

[美] Mark Breutzman　Tong Yi　审校

"十三五"国家重点图书

中国南方民间文学典籍英译丛书

丛书主编　张立玉　丛书副主编　起国庆

# MEIGE

出品单位：

中南民族大学南方少数民族文库翻译研究基地

云南省少数民族古籍整理出版规划办公室

WUHAN UNIVERSITY PRESS
武汉大学出版社

·汉英对照·

**图书在版编目(CIP)数据**

梅葛:汉英对照/云南省民族民间文学楚雄调查队搜集翻译整理; 邓之宇,张立玉英译.—武汉:武汉大学出版社,2021.3(2022.1重印)

中国南方民间文学典籍英译丛书/张立玉主编

"十三五"国家重点图书 2020年度国家出版基金资助项目

ISBN 978-7-307-21946-5

Ⅰ.梅… Ⅱ.①云… ②邓… ③张… Ⅲ.彝族—史诗—中国—汉、英 Ⅳ.I222.7

中国版本图书馆CIP数据核字(2020)第223104号

责任编辑:李晶晶 谢群英 责任校对:汪欣怡 版式设计:韩闻锦

出版发行:**武汉大学出版社** (430072 武昌 珞珈山)

(电子邮箱:cbs22@whu.edu.cn 网址:www.wdp.whu.edu.cn)

印刷:湖北恒泰印务有限公司

开本:720×1000 1/16 印张:27.75 字数:333千字

版次:2021年3月第1版 2022年1月第2次印刷

ISBN 978-7-307-21946-5 定价:75.00元

# 丛书编委会

**学术顾问**

王宏印　李正栓

**主编**

张立玉

**副主编**

起国庆

**编委会成员**（按姓氏笔画排列）

邓之宇　王向松　艾　芳　石定乐　龙江莉　刘　纯

陈兰芳　汤　茜　李克忠　杨　柳　杨筱奕　张立玉

张扬扬　张　瑛　和六花　依旺的　保俊萍　起国庆

陶开祥　鲁　钒　蔡　蔚　臧军娜

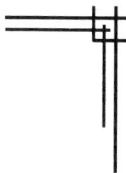

# 序

　　近年来，民族典籍英译捷报频传，硕果累累。韩家全教授等人的壮族系列经典翻译陆续出版，王宏印教授等人的系列民族典籍英译研究著作已经问世，李正栓教授等人的藏族格言诗英译著作不断在国内外出版，王维波教授等人的东北民族典籍英译著作纷纷付梓，李昌银教授等人的"云南少数民族经典作品英译文库"于2018年年底出版，其他民族典籍英译作品也在接踵而至。

　　近日，中南民族大学张立玉教授传来佳音：他们要出版"十三五"国家重点图书——"中国南方民间文学典籍英译丛书"。虽叫民间文学，其实基本上都是民族典籍。这一系列包括十本书，它们是：《黑暗传》《哭嫁歌》《哈尼阿培聪坡坡》《彝族民间故事》《南方民间创世神话选集》《十二奴局》《召树屯》《娥并与桑洛》《金笛》《梅葛》。其中，好几本是云南少数民族的。只有一本是汉族典籍，即《黑暗传》。很有意思的是，这些典籍展示了不同民族的创世史诗或诸如此类的东西。

　　《黑暗传》以民间歌谣唱本形象地描述了盘古开天辟地结束混沌黑暗，人类起源及社会发展的历程，融合了盘古、女娲、伏羲、炎帝神农氏、黄帝轩辕氏等众多英雄人物在洪荒时代艰难创世的一系列神话传说。它被称为汉族首部创世史诗。《哈尼阿培聪坡坡》是一部完整地记载哈尼族历史沿革的长篇史诗，堪称哈尼族的"史记"，长5000余行，以现实主义手法记叙了哈尼族祖先在各个历史时期的迁徙情况，并对其迁徙各地的原因、路线、途程，各个迁居地的社会生活、生产、风习、宗教，以及与毗邻民族的关系等，均作了详细而生动的辑录，因而该作品不仅具有文学价值，而且具有重大的历史学、社会学及宗教学价值。《南方民间创世神话选集》包括一些创世神话，主要是关于世界起源和人类起源的神话。《十二奴局》是一部在哈尼族广泛流传的民间诗歌，它通过"哈尼"（传统歌）的形式在民间演唱，世代流传。"奴局"是哈尼语，相当于汉族著述中的"篇"、"章"或汉族曲艺中的曲目。"十二奴局"即十二路歌的意思。译著表现了远古哈尼先民奇特的想象，涉及天体自然、人类发展、哈尼历史、历法计算、四时季令、农事活动等各个方面的知识，完整地反映了哈尼先民对天地形成、人类起源、民族迁徙的认识，具有创世神话与英雄史诗的合集之性质，可以说是哈尼族最为重要的文学经典之一。《梅葛》是彝族的一部长篇史诗，流传在云南省楚雄州的姚安、大姚等彝族地区。"梅葛"本为一种彝族歌调的名称，由于人们采用这种调子来唱彝族的创世史，因而创世史诗被称为"梅葛"。

其余几本书展示了一些少数民族的风俗习惯、恋爱故事、斗争故事等。《哭嫁歌》是土家族文化典籍。"哭嫁"是土家族姑娘在出嫁时进行的一种用歌声来诉说自己在封建买办婚姻制度下不幸命运的活动，指土家族姑娘的抒情歌谣，富有诗韵和乐感，融哀、怨、喜和乐为一体，以婉转的曲调向世人展示土家人独特的"哭"文化。《彝族民间故事》是一部以流传于云南楚雄彝族自治州彝族人民中间的民间故事为主体，同时覆盖全省包括小凉山等彝族地区的民间故事集。这些故事丰富多彩，从中能看到民族民间故事的各种形态和生动、奇妙而颇具彝族民族特色的文化特征。《召树屯》是傣族民间长篇叙事诗，叙述了傣族佛教世俗典籍《贝叶经·召树屯》中一个古老的传说故事。这部叙事诗一直为傣族人民所传唱，历久不衰。《娥并与桑洛》是一部优美生动的叙事

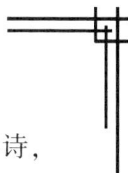

诗，一个凄美的爱情悲剧。《金笛》是一部苗族长篇叙事诗，富于变幻性和传奇性，尽情铺叙扎董丕冉与蒙诗彩奏的悲欢离合，热情赞颂他们在与魔虎的激烈斗争中所表现出来的坚贞不屈、英勇顽强的精神，许多情节含有浓郁的民族特色。

这些故事都很引人入胜，都很符合国家文化发展需求，向世人讲述中国故事，传播中华文化，并且讲述的是民族故事，充分体现了党和国家对各民族的关怀。

民族典籍英译是传播中国文化、文学和文明的重要途径，是中华文化"走出去"的重要组成部分，是国家战略，是提高文化"软实力"的重要方式，在文化交流和文明建设中起着不可或缺的作用，对提升中国国际话语权和构建中国对外话语体系以及对建设世界文学都有积极意义。

中国民族典籍使世界文化更加丰富多彩、绚丽多姿。我国各民族典籍中折射出的文化多样性极大地丰富了世界多元、特色鲜明的文化。人们对多样性形成全新的认识角度和思维方式，有助于开阔视野，丰富思考问题的角度，挖掘这些经典中的教育价值和文化价值，对世界其他民族都有指导和借鉴意义，并且有助于建设我国的文化自信。

民族典籍翻译与研究事业关乎国家的稳定统一，关乎民族关系的和谐发展，关乎世界多元文化的实现。在中国，民族典籍资源极为丰富，有待进一步挖掘、翻译，仍有许多少数民族典籍亟待拯救，民族典籍翻译与研究工作任重而道远，民族典籍翻译事业大有可为。

李正栓①

2019 年 7 月 19 日

---

① 李正栓，中国英汉语比较研究会典籍英译专业委员会常务副会长兼秘书长；中国中医药研究促进会传统文化翻译与国际传播专业委员会常务主任委员。

# 目　　录

# Contents

# 第一部　创　　世

## 一、开天辟地

远古的时候没有天，
远古的时候没有地。
要造天啦！
要造地啦！
哪个来造天？
哪个来造地？

格滋天神要造天，
他放下九个金果，
变成九个儿子。
九个儿子中，
五个来造天：
一个叫阿赌，
一个叫庶顽，
一个叫贪闹，

# Chapter One   The Genesis of the World

## Section One   The Creation of Sky and Earth

A long time ago there was no sky,

A long time ago there was no earth.

Ah! To make heaven!

Ah! To make earth!

Who would make sky?

Who would make earth?


Lord Gezi① would make sky.

Nine gold fruits he put down,

Nine sons they became.

Five sons among the nine,

Would make sky.

One son was called Gambling,

One son was called Rebellious,

One son was called Naughty,

---

① Gezi is the name of the lord.

一个叫顽连，
一个叫朵闹，
这是造天的儿子。

格滋天神要造地，
他放下七个银果，
变成七个姑娘。
七个姑娘中，
四个来造地：
一个叫扎则，
一个叫戳则，
一个叫慈则，
一个叫勤则，
这是造地的姑娘。

造天的儿子有啦！
造地的姑娘有啦！
造天的儿子没有衣裳穿，
拿云彩做衣裳；
造地的姑娘没有衣裳穿，
拿青苔做衣裳。

造天的儿子有啦！
造地的姑娘有啦！
造天的儿子没有粮吃，
拿露水当口粮；
造地的姑娘没有粮吃，
拿泥巴当口粮。

One son was called Disobedient,
One son was called Mischievous.
They were the five to make sky.

Lord Gezi would make earth.
Seven silver fruits he put down,
Seven daughters they became.
Four daughters among the seven
Would make earth.
One daughter was called Industrious,
One daughter was called Diligent,
One daughter was called Kindness,
One daughter was called Tireless.
They were the four to make earth.

Ah! The sons would make sky!
Ah! The daughters would make earth!
The sons were naked without clothes,
So clouds were taken to be worn.
The daughters were naked without clothes,
So moss was taken to put on.

Ah! The sons would make sky!
Ah! The daughters would make earth!
The sons were hungry without food,
So dew was taken to drink.
The daughters were hungry without food,
So mud was taken to eat.

吃的有啦!
穿的有啦!

造天没有模子,
造地没有模子。
天像一把伞,
地像一座轿。
拿伞做造天的模子,
拿轿做造地的模子。
蜘蛛网做天的底子,
蕨菜根做地的底子。

造天的五个儿子,
胆子有斗大,
个个喜欢赌钱,
个个喜欢玩闹。
大儿子守着赌,
大儿子守着玩;
二儿子躲着赌,
二儿子躲着玩;
三儿子跳着赌,
三儿子跳着玩;
四儿子把着赌,
四儿子把着玩;

Ah! They got things to eat!

Ah! They got things to wear!

Yet there was neither a mould to make sky,

Nor a mould to make earth.

Heaven looked like an umbrella,

And earth looked like a sedan chair.

An umbrella was used to shape the sky,

And a sedan chair was used to shape the earth.

Heaven was made from spider webs,

And earth was made from wild herb roots.

Those five sons who would make the sky

Were bold as brass.

Every one of them liked gambling,

Every one of them liked playing.

Number One son① gambled obsessively,

Number One son played obsessively.

Number Two son gambled secretly,

Number Two son played secretly.

Number Three son gambled excitedly,

Number Three son played excitedly.

Number Four son gambled fixatedly,

Number Four son played fixatedly.

---

①　First born son/daughter, second born son/daughter, third and so on are called differently in Chinese. Brothers or sisters are numbered off according to their age. This is a long tradition of the Chinese culture.

五儿子忙着赌，
五儿子忙着玩。
弟兄五个，
赌着来造天，
玩着来造天，
睡着来造天，
吃着来造天。
他们天天吃喝玩乐，
一天一天懒过去，
一天一天混过去。

造地的四个姑娘，
精心又细致，
个个喜欢造地，
个个喜欢劳动。
大姑娘飞快地做，
二姑娘甩团地做，
三姑娘手不停地做，
四姑娘顾不得吃饭地做。
姊妹四个，
忘了吃穿来造地，
忘了睡觉来造地，
不管天晴下雨来造地，
不分白天黑夜来造地，
耐耐心心地造地，
勤勤恳恳地造地。
一天一天过去，
一点一滴造成。

Number Five son gambled attentively,

Number Five son played attentively.

Those five sons made sky,

While gambling,

While playing,

While sleeping,

While eating.

They indulged themselves every single day,

While being idle,

While being lazy.


Those four daughters who would make earth

Were meticulous and conscientious.

Every one of them liked earth-making,

Every one of them liked working.

Number One daughter worked quickly,

Number Two daughter worked swiftly,

Number Three daughter worked avidly,

Number Four daughter worked devotedly.

Those four sisters made earth,

Even skipping meals

And sleep.

Those four sisters were making earth both in sunny and rainy

days,

Those four sisters were making earth days and nights.

They were making earth patiently,

They were making earth dedicatedly.

As time went by,

Earth took its shape little by little.

过了很久很久，
五兄弟把天造好了，
四姊妹把地造好了。
不知道天有多大，
不知道地有多大。
要量天啦！
要量地啦！
请什么来量天？
请什么来量地？

请飞蛾来量天，
请蜻蜓来量地，
天上量一量，
地下量一量，

天有七拃，
地有九拃，
天造小了，
地造大了，
天盖地呀盖不合。
弟兄五个不在意，
放心去玩耍；
姊妹四个心着急，
恐怕天神来责骂。

A long long time later,

Five brothers finally made the sky,

Four sisters eventually made the earth.

No one knew the size of the sky,

No one knew the size of the earth.

Ah! To measure the sky!

Ah! To measure the earth!

Who would measure the sky?

Who would measure the earth?


Moths were invited to measure the sky,

Dragonflies were invited to measure the earth,


Ah! To measure the sky!

Ah! To measure the earth!


The sky was seven Pai①,

The earth was nine Pai.

The sky was made small,

While the earth was made big.

Alas! The sky was not able to cover the earth.

Five brothers were not concerned about this,

And they continued to have fun and indulge themselves.

Four sisters took it seriously,

And they were afraid of being scolded by Lord Gezi.

---

① Pai: a measure unit of length in ancient time, referring to the
length between two stretched arms.

格滋天神知道了，
告诉四姊妹：
"不要心焦，
不要害怕，
地做大了，
有人会缩；
天做小了，
有人会拉。
地缩小，
天拉大，
天就能盖地啦！"
阿夫会缩地，
阿夫会拉天。
请阿夫的三个儿子，
抓住天边往下拉，
把天拉得大又凹。

放三对麻蛇来缩地，
麻蛇围着地边箍拢来，
地面分出了高低，
地边还箍得不齐；
放三对蚂蚁咬地边，
把地边咬得整整齐齐。
放三对野猪来拱地，
放三对大象来拱地，

When Lord Gezi heard about this,

He comforted his four daughters:

"Do not worry,

Do not panic,

If earth is made too big,

It will be shrunk.

If sky is made too small,

It will be stretched.

Alas! The earth will be shrunk,

And the sky will be stretched,

The sky will be able to cover the earth."

Lord Fu① could shrink earth,

Lord Fu could stretch sky.

His three sons came for help.

They dragged the sky's edge downward,

Hence making the sky arch-like and wider.


Three pairs of snakes came to shrink earth,

They squeezed the earth from all sides,

Hence creating mountains and ravines of all heights,

Though making earth's uneven edges.

Three pairs of ants came to gnaw,

Hence making the edges neat and tidy.

Three pairs of wild boars, with their snout, came to dig the earth,

Three pairs of elephants, with their trunk, came to dig the earth.

---

① Fu is the name of the lord.

拱了七十七昼夜，
有了山来有了箐，
有了平坝有了河。
天拉大了，
地缩小了，
这样合适啦，
天地相合啦。

不知天牢不牢，
不知地牢不牢。
要试天啦！
要试地啦！
打雷来试天，
地震来试地。
试天天开裂，
试地地通洞。

天开裂要补起来，
地通洞要补起来。
格滋天神叫五个儿子补天，
格滋天神叫四个姑娘补地。
用松毛做针，
蜘蛛网做线，
云彩做补丁，
把天补起来。
用老虎草做针，
酸绞藤做线，
地公叶子做补丁，
把地补起来。

14

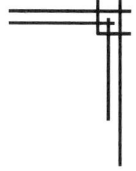

After digging for seventy-seven days and nights,

Hills and valleys were created,

Flatlands and rivers were created.

The sky was stretched,

The earth was shrunk,

Ah! Now they would match,

Ah! Now the sky would cover the earth.


No one knew whether the sky was firm,

No one knew whether the earth was firm.

Ah! To test the sky!

Ah! To test the earth!

Thunder will test the sky,

Earthquake will test the earth.

Thunder made the sky crack,

Earthquakes made the earth full of holes.


Sky's cracks needed patching up,

Earth's holes needed filling.

Lord Gezi asked his five sons to patch up the sky,

Lord Gezi asked his four daughters to fill the earth.

Taking pine leaves as needles,

Taking spider webs as threads,

Taking clouds as patches,

They patched the sky.

Taking rockfoil stems as needles,

Taking grape vines as threads,

Taking blindweed leaves as fillers,

They filled the earth.

天补好了，
地补好了。
打雷时天不会垮，
地震时地不会塌，
可是补好的天还在摆，
补好的地还在摇。
因为没有撑天的柱，
没有撑地的柱，
要找撑天的柱，
要找撑地的柱。

格滋天神说：
"水里面有鱼，
世间的东西要算鱼最大。
公鱼三千斤，
母鱼七百斤。
捉公鱼去！
捉母鱼去！
公鱼捉来撑地角，
母鱼捉来撑地边。"

公鱼不眨眼，
大地不会动；
母鱼不翻身，
大地不会摇。
地的四角撑起来，
大地稳实了。

Then the sky was patched,

And the earth was filled.

Sky will not crack in thunder,

Earth will not collapse in earthquakes.

But the repaired sky was still shaking,

While the repaired earth was still trembling.

Because there were no pillars

To hold the sky and to support the earth,

Pillars were needed

To hold the sky and to support the earth.


Lord Gezi said,

"There are fish in water.

A fish is the biggest thing on earth.

A male fish weighs 1,500 kilograms,

And a female fish weighs 350 kilograms.

Go catch a male fish!

Go catch a female fish!

A male fish will bolster earth's edges,

A female fish will bolster earth's corners."


The male fish did not blink its eyes,

And the earth did not move a bit.

The female fish did not turn over,

And the earth did not shake a bit.

The four edges of the earth were bolstered up,

The earth should be stable and firm.

大地撑住了，
大地稳实了。
没有撑天柱，
天还在摇摆。
格滋天神说：
"山上有老虎，
世间的东西要算虎最猛。
引老虎去！
哄老虎去！
用虎的脊梁骨撑天心，
用虎的脚杆骨撑四边。"

造天五弟兄，
胆子有斗大！
他们会撑山，
他们去引虎。

手中紧握大铁伞，
伞把装上铁弯钩。
十二架山梁上引一引，
老虎张着大嘴走出来，
老虎抖着身子走出来，
老虎被引出来啦。
老虎张着血盆大口奔来，
老虎抖着斑斓的身子扑来。
造天五弟兄，
忙把伞撑开，

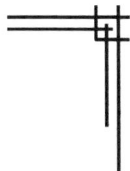

The earth was held up,

The earth was stable and firm.

Yet there were no pillars to hold the sky,

And the sky was still shaking.

Lord Gezi said,

"There are tigers on mountains,

And tigers are the most ferocious creatures on earth,

Go draw a tiger out!

Go coax a tiger out!

A tiger's backbone can support sky's center,

A tiger's shin bone can support sky's edge."


The five brothers who made the sky

Were as bold as a lion!

They searched in the deep mountains,

They drew a tiger out.


They firmly held iron umbrellas,

Umbrella handles had iron hooks.

They searched twelve mountain ridges,

And finally saw a tiger walking out.

His mouth was widely open and his body moved briskly.

Ah! The tiger was drawn out!

The tiger pounced with its mouth wide-open,

The tiger leaped with its striped body,

The five brothers

Opened their umbrellas quickly,

挡住了老虎，
钩住了老虎。
老虎被哄住啦！
老虎被钩住啦！

山草掺上棕，
棕毛掺山草，
索子搓出来，
不能多一拿，
不能少一拿，
索子搓成十二拿，
牵着老虎走回来。

猛虎杀死了，
大家来分虎。
四根大骨莫要分，
四根大骨做撑天的柱子；
肩膀莫要分，
肩膀做东南西北方向。
把天撑起来了，
天也稳实了。

天上没有太阳，
天上没有月亮，
天上没有星星，
天上没有白云彩，
天上没有红云彩，
天上没有虹，
天上什么也没有。

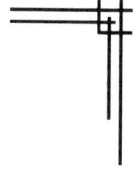

Blocked the tiger firmly,
And hooked the tiger tightly.
Ah! The tiger was hooked!
Ah! The tiger was caught!

Palm fiber was mixed with mountain grass,
Mountain grass was blended with palm fiber,
Together they were twisted into a rope.
The rope should be in the length of twelve Pai,
No more,
No less.
The rope would be used to haul the tiger back.

The fierce tiger was killed,
Everyone came for one share.
The four big bones of the tiger should not be taken,
They would be the four pillars to hold the sky.
The shoulders of the tiger should not be taken,
They would point the four directions.
The sky was held up finally,
And it was stable and firm.

There was no sun in the sky,
There was no moon in the sky,
There were no stars in the sky,
There were no white clouds in the sky,
There were no red clouds in the sky,
There were no rainbows in the sky,
There was nothing in the sky.

地上没有树木，
地上没有树根，
地上没有大江，
地上没有大海，
地上没有飞禽，
地上没有走兽，
地上什么也没有。

虎头莫要分，
虎头做天头。
虎尾莫要分，
虎尾做地尾。
虎鼻莫要分，
虎鼻做天鼻。
虎耳莫要分，
虎耳做天耳。

虎眼莫要分，
左眼做太阳，
右眼做月亮。
虎须莫要分，
虎须做阳光。
虎牙莫要分，
虎牙做星星。
虎油莫要分，
虎油做云彩。
虎气莫要分，
虎气成雾气。

There were no tree trunks on the earth,

There were no tree roots on the earth,

There were no rivers on the earth,

There were no oceans on the earth,

There were no birds on the earth,

There were no beasts on the earth,

There was nothing on the earth.


The head of the tiger should not be taken,

It turned into the head of the sky.

The tail of the tiger should not be taken,

It turned into the tail of the earth.

The nose of the tiger should not be taken,

It turned into the nose of the sky.

The ears of the tiger should not be taken,

They turn into the ears of the sky.


The eyes of the tiger should not be taken,

The left eye turned into the sun,

The right eye turned into the moon.

The whiskers of the tiger should not be taken,

They turned into sunshine.

The teeth of the tiger should not be taken,

They turned into stars.

The fat of the tiger should not be taken,

It turned into clouds.

The breath of the tiger should not be taken,

It turned into mist.

虎心莫要分，
虎心做天心地胆。
虎肚莫要分，
虎肚做大海。
虎血莫要分，
虎血做海水。

大肠莫要分，
大肠变大江。
小肠莫要分，
小肠变成河。
排骨莫要分，
排骨做道路。

虎皮莫要分，
虎皮做地皮。
硬毛莫要分，
硬毛变树林。
软毛莫要分，
软毛变成草。
细毛莫要分，
细毛做秧苗。

骨髓莫要分，
骨髓变金子。
小骨头莫要分，
小骨头变银子。
虎肺莫要分，
虎肺变成铜。

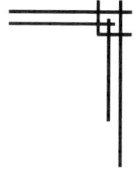

The heart of the tiger should not be taken,
It turned into the heart of sky and earth.
The belly of the tiger should not be taken,
It turned into oceans.
The blood of the tiger should not be taken,
It turned into seawater.

The large intestine of the tiger should not be taken,
It turned into great rivers,
The small intestine of the tiger should not be taken,
It turned into small streams.
The ribs of the tiger should not be taken,
They turned into paths and roads.

The skin of the tiger should not be taken,
It turned into earth surface.
The bristles of the tiger should not be taken,
They turned into forests.
The fur of the tiger should not be taken,
It turned into grass.
The fuzz of the tiger should not be taken,
It turned into seedlings.

The bone marrow of the tiger should not be taken,
It turned into gold.
The tiny bones of the tiger should not be taken,
They turned into sliver.
The lungs of the tiger should not be taken,
They turned into copper.

虎肝莫要分，
虎肝变成铁。
脾莫要分，
脾变成锡。
腰子莫要分，
腰子做磨石。

大虱子变成老水牛，
小虱子变成黑猪黑羊，
虱子蛋变成绵羊，
头皮变成雀鸟。

最后分虎肉，
虎肉分成十二份，
一份也不多，
一份也不少。

给老鸦一份，
老鸦吃了喜欢。
"呱！呱！呱！"
漫山遍野叫。

给喜鹊一份，
喜鹊吃了也喜欢。
"啾！啾！啾！"
飞去踩秧田。

The liver of the tiger should not be taken,
It turned into iron.
The spleen of the tiger should not be taken,
It turned into tin.
The kidneys of the tiger should not be taken,
They turned into millstones.

The big lice on the tiger's body turned into old buffalos,
Those small lice turned into black pigs and goats,
The lice eggs turned into sheep,
The hair of the lice turned into sparrows and other birds.

The flesh of the tiger
Was divided into twelve portions,
No more,
No less.

Crows got one portion,
They ate it and were satisfied.
"Caw-caw-caw!"
They cawed over the hills.

Magpies got one portion,
They ate it and were satisfied.
"Jiu-Jiu-Jiu!"①
They stamped the paddy fields with their feet.

---

① Sounds made by magpies.

竹鸡分一份,
竹鸡吃了也喜欢。
"好着着!好着着!"
叫着飞了过去。

野鸡分一份,
野鸡吃了也喜欢
"嗦呼呼!嗦呼呼!"
叫着飞了过去。

老豺狗分一份,
吃了去拖猪,
吃了去拖羊,
叫着跑上山去。

画眉分一份,
画眉吃了心喜欢。
"叽里里!叽里里!"
叫着飞了过去。

黄蚊子分一份,
黄蚊子吃了喜欢。
"天黄!地黄!"
叫着飞了过去。

Bamboo partridges got one portion,
They ate it and were satisfied.
"Hao-zuo-zuo! Hao-zuo-zuo!"①
They cried and flew away.

Pheasants got one portion,
They ate it and were satisfied.
"Sou-hu-hu! Sou-hu-hu!"②
They cried and flew off into the distance.

Jackals got one portion,
They ate it,
And went to catch pigs and sheep.
They cried and ran into the hills.

Thrushes got one portion,
They ate it and were satisfied.
"Ji-li-li, Ji-li-li!"③
They cried and flew off into the distance.

Yellow mosquitos got one portion,
They ate it and were satisfied.
"Tian-huang! Di-huang!"④
They cried and flew away.

---

① Sounds made by bamboo partridges.
② Sounds made by pheasants.
③ Sounds made by thrushes.
④ Literally means, yellowish sky and yellowish earth.

黄蜂分一份，
黄蜂分着了心喜欢。

葫芦蜂分一份，
葫芦蜂分着了心喜欢。

老土蜂分一份，
老土蜂分着了心喜欢。

大蚊子分一份，
大蚊子分着了心喜欢。

绿头苍蝇分一份，
绿头苍蝇吃了心喜欢。

饿老鹰没有分着，
饿老鹰呀心不甘。
一飞飞上天，
伸开了翅膀，
遮住了太阳。

天变成黑压压一团，
地变成黑乌乌一团，
再也分不出白天，
再也分不出夜晚。

哪个能治饿老鹰？
绿头苍蝇能治饿老鹰。

Hornets got one portion,
They were delighted.

Bumblebees got one portion,
They were delighted.

Wasps got one portion,
They were delighted.

Big mosquitos got one portion,
They were delighted.

Blowflies got one portion,
They ate it and were delighted.

But the hungry eagle got no portion,
And he was angry.
It spread its wings,
And soared up into the sky,
Shutting out the sun.

The sky turned dark,
The earth turned dark,
People could not distinguish,
Whether it was day or night.

Who could tackle the hungry eagle?
The blowflies could tackle the hungry eagle.

绿头苍蝇飞上天，
落在老鹰翅膀上，
密密麻麻下了子。

过了三天，
过了三夜，
老鹰翅膀生了蛆，
翅膀生蛆跌下来。
太阳发亮啦！

有了白天啦！

老鹰掉在地上，
把地遮了一半，
还是只有黑夜，
还是没有白天。

请谁抬老鹰？
蚂蚁抬老鹰。
老鹰抬开了，
昼夜分出来。

有白天啦！
有黑夜啦！
天亮太阳出来啦！
天黑月亮出来啦！

They flew up into the sky,

Landed on the eagle's wings,

And layed eggs densely there.


Three days passed,

Three nights passed.

Maggots covered the eagle's wings.

Those infested wings failed the eagle.

Ah! The sun came out again!


Ah! Bright day came again!


The eagle fell down to the ground,

With its body covering half of the earth.

Dark night came again,

With no bright day anymore.


Who could move the eagle away?

Ants could move it away.

The eagle was then moved away,

Days and nights could be distinguished again.


Ah! Days came back!

Ah! Nights came back!

The sun rose during the day!

The moon rose during the night!

## 二、人类起源

天造成了，
地造成了，
万物有了，
昼夜分开了，
就是没有人，
格滋天神来造人。

天上撒下三把雪，
落地变成三代人。
撒下第一把是第一代，
撒下第二把是第二代，
撒下第三把是第三代。

头把撒下独脚人，
只有一尺二寸长；
独自一人不会走，
两人手搂脖子快如飞；
吃的饭是泥土，
下饭菜是沙子。
月亮照着活得下去，

# Section Two   The Origin of Human Beings

The sky was made,

The earth was made,

The creatures were made,

Days and nights were distinguished,

But human beings had not yet been made,

So Lord Gezi decided to make them.


He scattered three handfuls of snow,

Each of them became one generations of people.

The first one turned into the first generation,

The second one turned into the second generation,

The third one turned into the third generation.


The first handful of snow became one-legged people

Whose height was only one Chi① and two Cun②.

The one-legged people were not able to walk alone.

Putting arms around each other's neck,

One pair of them could walk together as fast as the wind.

They ate mud and soil,

They ate sand and gravel,

They lived under moonlight,

---

① Measure unit for height. 1 Chi equals 33. 3 centimeters.

② Measure unit for height. 1 Cun equals 3.33 centimeters. 10 Cun equals 1 Chi.

太阳晒着活不下去，
这代人无法生存，
这代人被晒死了。

撒下第二把，
人有一丈三尺长，
没有衣裳，
没有裤子，
拿树叶做衣裳，
拿树叶做裤子，
这才有了衣裳，
这才有了裤子。

没有水，
没有火，
没有吃的，
没有住的，
吃的山林果，
住的老山洞。

没有春夏秋冬，
不分四季四时；
天上有九个太阳，
天上有九个月亮；
白天太阳晒，
晚上月亮照；

But could not live under sunlight.

This generation could not survive,

And died in the sun.


The second handful of snow became people

Whose height was one Zhang① and three Chi,

They had no clothes to wear,

They had no pants to wear.

They took leaves to make clothes,

They took leaves to make pants,

Clothes and pants started to exist

From that time on.


There was no water,

There was no fire,

There was no food to eat,

There were no houses to live in.

They took mountain fruits as foods,

They took mountain caves as shelters.


There were no seasons,

There was no spring, summer, autumn or winter.

There were nine suns above the sky,

And there were nine moons above the sky.

Nine suns were burning during the day,

---

① Measure unit for height. 1 Zhang equals 3.33 meters. 1 Zhang equals 10 Chi.

晚上过得去，
白天过不去。
牛骨头晒焦了，
斑鸠毛晒掉了。
做着活计瞌睡来，
一睡睡了几百年，
身上长青苔，
这代人活不下去，
这代人也晒死了。

格滋天神，
左手拿錾，
右手拿锤，
来錾太阳，
来錾月亮，
留一个太阳在天上，
留一个月亮在天上。
太阳落在阿娃西山，
月亮落在菠萝西山，
四季分出来，
草皮树根长起来。

撒下第三把，
人的两只眼睛朝上生。

And nine moons were shining during the night.

They could live under moonlight,

But they could not live under sunlight.

Cattle bones were scorched,

Bird feathers were singed.

They fell asleep while doing work,

And slept for hundreds of years,

With moss growing on their bodies.

This generation could not survive,

And again died in the sun.


Lord Gezi came,

With a chisel in his left hand,

And a hammer in his right hand.

He chiseled suns away,

He chiseled moons away,

Leaving only one sun and one moon

Above the sky.

The remaining sun set over the west of Mount Awa①,

The moon went down behind the west of Mount Boluo②,

Then four seasons could be distinguished,

Then grass and roots could grow.


The third handful of snow

Became people with straight-upward eyes.

① Mountain names.
② Mountain names.

格滋天神，
撒三把苦荞，
撒在米拉山；
撒三把谷子，
撒在石山岭；
撒三把麦子，
撒在寿延山。
麦子出穗了，
谷子出穗了，
荞子长出来了。

没有火，
天上老龙想办法，
三串小火镰，
一打两头着，
从此人类有了火。
什么都有了，
日子好过了。

这代人的心不好，
他们不耕田不种地，
他们不薅草不拔草。
看见田里没有牙齿草，
铲铲地皮就放水，
白天睡在田边，

Lord Gezi scattered three handfuls of buckwheat

On Mount Mila①;

Lord Gezi scattered three handfuls of millet

On Mount Shishan②;

Lord Gezi scattered three handfuls of wheat

On Mount Shouyan③.

Wheat started to send up ears,

Millet started to send up ears,

Buckwheat started to grow.


There was no fire.

The old dragon in heaven came up with an idea.

He took three sets of flint sickle, struck them,

And produced fire on both ends.

People got fire from that time on.

People had everything,

And they started to live a better-off life.


However, people of this generation had no good hearts,

They did no plowing or seeding,

They did no weeding or trimming.

Seeing no plant in fields,

They only shoveled the soil and watered it.

They slept in fields during the day,

---

① Mountain names.

② Mountain names.

③ Mountain names.

夜晚睡在地角，
一天到晚，
吃饭睡觉，
睡觉吃饭。

天神问他们：
"为何不耕不种？
为何不薅不拔？"
"田里不长牙齿草。
没有活计做。"

格滋天神手一撒，
甘香树叶落地下，
田里长了牙齿草。
直眼睛的人，
从此要栽种，
从此要薅草。

这代人的心不好，
糟蹋五谷粮食，
谷子拿去打埂子，
麦粑粑拿去堵水口，
用苦荞面、甜荞面糊墙。

格滋天神看不过：
"不该这样来糟蹋！
这代人的心不好，
这代人要换一换。"

And slept on farmland during the night.

On and on,

They ate and slept,

Doing nothing.


Lord Gezi asked them:

"Why do not you plow and seed?

Why do not you trim and weed?"

The answer was:

"There are no plants in the farmland and there is no work to

do."


Lord Gezi scattered a handful of sweet leaves,

And those leaves fell down on the farmland.

Plants started to grow on lands.

People with straight-upward eyes

Had to go plow and seed from that time on,

And had to do weeding and trimming from that time on.


People of this generation had no good hearts,

And they wasted grain and wheat.

They built farmland ridges with grain,

They blocked outfalls with wheat cakes,

They pasted walls with buckwheat dough.


Lord Gezi could not bear it:

"Food should not be wasted.

People of this generation have no good hearts,

They have to be replaced."

格滋天神派武姆勒娃下凡来，
派他把第三代人换一换，
武姆勒娃变只大老熊，
堵水漫金山。
寻找好人种，
留下传人烟。

直眼人学博若，
有五个儿子，
有一个姑娘。
弟兄五个人，
山上犁生地，
箐底开水田。
今天犁好的，
明天被老熊翻回来；
明天犁好的，
后天被老熊翻回来。
整整犁了三天地，
三天都被老熊翻回来。

五弟兄来商议，
五弟兄想办法：
到地头下一个扣，
到地中下一个扣，
到地尾下一个扣。
锄头做踩板，

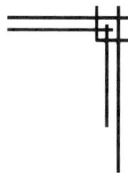

Lord Gezi sent Lord Wumulewa[①] to the earth,

And asked him to replace people of this generation.

Lord Wumulewa transformed into a big old bear,

Whose huge body blocked the water and flood the earth.

He wanted to seek a good person

To start a new generation.


There was a person named Xueboruo,

He had five sons

And one daughter.

These five brothers

Were plowing new fields on hills,

And opening up paddy fields in the valleys.

The field they finished plowing in one day,

Would be flattened by the bear the next day.

The field they finished plowing the next day,

Would be flattened by the bear the day after.

They had plowed the field for three days,

And each day the field was flattened by the bear.


Five brothers had a meeting,

They came up with an idea.

One trap was set in one end of the field,

One trap in the center,

And one trap in the other end.

A hoe head was taken as a pedal,

---

① Lord Wumulewa: a deity in Yi culture.

锄把做夹弓，
犁头做横担，
耕索做扣绳，
犁杆做扣杆，
犁耳做扣梢，
犁头做扣环。
老熊到地里，
踩到扣子上，
老熊被套住了，
老熊被拴住了。

学博若的大儿子来串地，
看见捉住大老熊，
心里很高兴。
"学博若的大儿子，
你来替我解一解。"

大儿子不愿解：
"我白天犁好的地，
你夜里来翻平，
你的心不好，
就是要捉你，
我不替你解，
我要去攀山。"

学博若的二儿子来串地，
看见捉住大老熊，
心里很高兴。

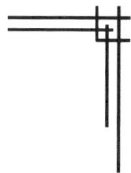

A hoe handle was taken as a bow,

A plow beam was taken as a pole arm,

A plow rope was taken as the rope to trap,

A plow brace was taken as the trap's rod,

A plow share was taken as the trap's bolt,

A plow clevis was taken as the trap's ring.

When the bear came to the field,

He stepped on the trap,

The bear was trapped,

He was caught.


Number One son of Xueboruo came to the field,

And saw that the bear was caught.

He was very delighted.

"Number One son of Xueboruo,

Please come to release me."


Number One son was not willing to and he said,

"I plowed the field during the day,

And you flattened it during the night.

You do not have a kind heart,

And you deserve to be caught.

I will go hunting now,

And will not release you."


Number Two son of Xueboruo came to the field,

and saw that the bear was caught.

He was very delighted.

"学博若的二儿子，
你来替我解。"

二儿子不愿解：
"你的心不好，
就是要捉你，
我不得闲解，
我要去放羊。"

学博若的三儿子来串地，
看见捉住大老熊，
心里很高兴。
"学博若的三儿子，
你来替我解一解。"

三儿子不愿解：
"你的心不好，
就是要捉你，
我不替你解，
我要去放牛。"

学博若的四儿子来串地，
看见捉住大老熊，
心里很高兴。
"学博若的四儿子，
你来替我解一解。"

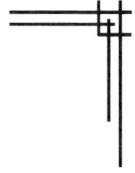

"Number Two son of Xueboruo,
Please come to release me."

Number Two son was not willing to and he said,
"You do not have a kind heart,
And you deserve to be caught.
I will go tend to the sheep now,
And will not release you."

Number Three son of Xueboruo came to the field,
and saw that the bear was caught.
He was very delighted.
"Number Three son of Xueboruo,
Please come to release me."

Number Three son was not willing to and he said,
"You do not have a kind heart,
And you deserve to be caught.
I will go tend to the cattle now,
And will not release you."

Number Four son of Xueboruo came to the field,
and saw that the bear was caught.
He was very delighted.
"Number Four son of Xueboruo,
Please come to release me."

四儿子不愿解：
"你的心不好，
就是要捉你，
我不得闲解，
我要去犁生地。"

四弟兄都喊打，
四弟兄都喊杀。

学博若的小儿子，
背着小妹跑过来：
"看它的头像祖父，
看它的身子像祖母，
千万不能打，
千万不能杀。"

"学博若的小儿子，
你来替我解一解。"

小儿子想去解，
心里怪害怕。

"心里别害怕，
若是救了我，
我要给你一句话。"

学博若的小儿子，
解开绳索，

Number Four son was not willing to and he said,
"You do not have a kind heart,
And you deserve to be caught.
I will go plow the field now,
And will not release you."

The four brothers all wanted to punish the bear,
The four brothers all wanted to kill the bear.

The youngest son of Xueboruo came to the field,
Carrying his little sister on his back.
"His head looks like our grandfather's,
His body looks like our grandmother's.
We cannot punish him,
We cannot kill him."

"The youngest son of Xueboruo,
Please come to release me."

The youngest son wanted to release him,
But he was afraid.

"Do not be afraid,
If you release me,
I will tell you something."

The youngest son of Xueboruo
Untied the rope,

搭下木梯，
救了武姆勒娃。

武姆勒娃说：
"人心很不好，
要换人种了，
水要漫金山，
大水快发了。
大哥打金柜，
二哥打银柜，
三哥打铜柜，
四哥打铁柜，
你们四弟兄，
赶快躲进柜。

"小弟弟你良心好，
给你三颗葫芦籽，
赶快回去栽葫芦。

"正月初一那一天，
最好这天栽葫芦，
正月栽下葫芦籽，
三天要浇一次水；
栽下三天会出芽，
过了三天藤就爬；
又过三天开白花，
再过三天结葫芦，
最后三天会长大。

And offered him a ladder to get off.

He saved Lord Wumulewa.


Lord Wumulewa said,

"People of this generation have no good hearts,

And they have to be replaced.

Water will flood the world,

The flood will inundate the world.

Your Number One brother needs to make a gold cabinet,

Your Number Two brother needs to make a silver cabinet,

Your Number Three brother needs to make a copper cabinet,

Your Number Four brother needs to make an iron cabinet,

Your four brothers,

Can hide in those cabinets afterwards.


"You have a kind heart,

And I will give you three gourd seeds.

Go back home to plant them immediately.


"The first day of the new year

Will be the perfect day to plant the seeds.

You plant them in the first month,

And water them every three days.

It will grow a bud after three days,

It will grow a vine after another three days,

It will grow a white flower after another three days,

It will grow a gourd after another three days,

This gourd will be fully grown in last three days.

"葫芦藤有牛粗，
葫芦叶有簸箕大，
结了一个独葫芦，
葫芦结得像囤子。

"你不要干着急，
你不要瞎猜想，
不是有妖精，
不是有妖怪，
葫芦结饱了，
摘得葫芦了。

"大理出小刀，
是开葫芦的刀。
用高山的松香封住葫芦口，
箐底的黄蜡糊住葫芦口；
你兄妹搬进葫芦里，
饿了就吃葫芦籽。"

四弟兄听了武姆勒娃的话，
大哥打好了金柜；
二哥打好了银柜；
三哥打好了铜柜；
四哥打好了铁柜。
弟兄四人找住处，
找好住处杀老熊。

"The stems of the gourd are as thick as a carrying-pole,
The leaves of the gourd are as broad as a dustpan.
The gourd is as big as a basket,
And this gourd is the unique one.

"Do not worry,
Do not be afraid.
It is not a monster,
It is not an evil spirit.
When the gourd is fully grown,
You can harvest it.

"Dali① is famous for pocketknives,
And those pocketknives are perfect to cut the gourd open.
Use rosin from high mountain to seal the gourd's mouth,
Use yellow beeswax from deep valley to seal gourd's mouth.
You and your sister will live in the gourd,
And you can eat seeds of gourd when you are hungry."

Four brothers listened to Lord Wumulewa,
Number One brother made a gold cabinet,
Number Two brother made a silver cabinet,
Number Three brother made a copper cabinet,
Number Four brother made an iron cabinet.
When the shelters were ready,
Four brothers killed the bear.

---

①　Name of a region in Yunnan Province of China. There is a large population of Yi people living in this region.

老熊的鲜血淌成河，
尸体漂河中，
脑袋顺水淌，
淌入东洋海，
塞住出水洞，
水就涨起来。

狂风和暴雨，
越淹越厉害，
水声隆隆波浪翻，
普天之下都淹完。

学博若的四个儿子，
先闸一道围，
水涨到山腰。
再筑一道围，
水淹过了金山。

学博若的四个儿子，
躲进柜子里，
金柜银柜沉下水，
铜柜铁柜沉下水。

洪水滚滚接着天，
海鱼吃了天上的星星，
螃蟹也在天上跑，
白天黑夜分不清，
只有水声风浪声。

The blood of the bear flowed into a river,

His corpse floated in the river,

It floated down the river head-first,

Finally blocked the drainage hole,

Where the river merged into east sea.

Hence the river overflowed.


With wild wind and rainstorms,

The flood became more severe.

Water was tumbling and waves rolling,

The whole world was flooded entirely.


Four sons of Xueboruo built a first dam,

But water could not be blocked,

And reached half the mountain high.

They built a second dam,

But water could not be blocked and flooded the Golden Mountain.


Four sons of Xueboruo

Hid in their cabinets.

Gold cabinet and silver cabinet sank into the water,

Copper cabinet and iron cabinet sank into the water.


Water roared and reached up to the sky,

Fish ate stars in the sky,

And crabs scuttled in the sky.

Days and nights could not be distinguished,

Only sounds of wind and tide could be heard.

洪水淹了七十七昼夜，
天神着了慌，
下凡来车水。
东方指一指，
山头现出来；
南方指一指，
树木草根看见了；
西方指一指，
水退到河边；
北方指一指，
水退到河底；
中间指一指，
水全干了。

人种没有了，
人种死光了。

天神站在山头上，
看不见一只飞鸟，
听不到一点声音，
格滋天神找人种，
四面八方走。

找到岔路口，
遇着葫芦蜂：
"葫芦蜂，葫芦蜂！
你是好蜂子，
你若有好心，

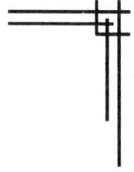

The flood lasted seventy-seven days and nights,

Even Lord Gezi started to get worried,

He came down to the human world to control the flood.

When he pointed to the east,

Mountain tops appeared.

When he pointed to the south,

Tree and grass came into sight.

When he pointed to the west,

Water retreated to the river bank.

When he pointed to the north,

Water receded to the riverbed.

When he pointed to the center,

Water dried up to the bottom.


People all died out,

And the human race was extinct.


Lord Gezi stood at the mountain top,

But he did not see any flying birds

And did not hear any sounds.

Lord Gezi walked around in all directions,

Trying to find human beings.


At a crossroads,

He met a bumblebee:

"Bumblebee, Bumblebee,

You are a good bee,

If you are kind,

请你告诉我，
你看见人种没有？"

"人种我没见，
要是遇着了，
我要叮死他。"

天神发了怒，
打它一鞭子，
蜂腰打断了，
蜂子大声叫：
"接好我的腰，
我就告诉你。"

扯根马尾接蜂腰，
蜂腰一接好，
蜂子飞跑了。
格滋天神骂道：
"七月葫芦八月包，
你养娃娃吊着养，
九月十月放火烧。"

天神找人种，
山山箐箐跑，
遇着小松树：

Please tell me,

Have you ever seen any human being?"

"I have not seen any human being,

If I met any,

I would sting them to death."

Lord Gezi got angry,

And flogged it with a whip.

Bumblebee's waist was broken,

And it shouted out loudly:

"If you fix my waist,

I will tell you."

Lord Gezi twitched a horsetail-hair,

And used it to fix the bumblebee's waist.

But the bumblebee flew away immediately.

Lord Gezi swore at it furiously:

"Your honeycomb will look like the gourd in July and August,

Your babies will be raised only in honeycomb hanging in trees,

And people will have them burned in September and October."

Lord Gezi walked around all mountains and valleys,

Trying to find human beings.

He met a little pine:

"小松树，小松树！
你是好树子，
你若有好心，
请你告诉我，
你看见人种没有？"

"人种我没见，
要是遇着了，
我的叶子硬，
戳也戳死他。"

天神发怒了，
一鞭打下去，
松树成三杈。
格滋天神骂道：
"等到人种找着了，
人烟旺起来，
砍你一棵绝一棵。"

天神找人种，
跑到山梁上，
遇着罗汉松：
"罗汉松，罗汉松！
你是好树子，
你若有好心，
请你告诉我，
你看见人种没有？"

"Little pine, little pine,

You are a good pine,

If you are kind,

Please tell me,

Have you ever seen any human being?"


"I have not seen any human being,

If I met any,

I would use my hard needles

To poke them to death."


Lord Gezi got angry,

And flogged it with a whip.

The pine split into three.

Lord Gezi swore at it furiously:

"When I find a human being,

I will let them reproduce.

If people cut you down, you will never grow again."


Lord Gezi climbed to the mountain ridge,

Trying to find human beings.

He met a Buddhist pine:

"Buddhist pine, Buddhist pine,

You are a good tree,

If you are kind,

Please tell me,

Have you ever seen any human being?"

"刮了三次春风，
下了三场春雨，
人种没看见，
要是见了人，
我的叶子密，
给他来避风，
替他来遮雨。"

天神好喜欢，
封赠罗汉松：
"罗汉松，是好树，
等到人种找到了，
人烟旺起来，
砍你一棵发百棵。"

天神找人种，
找到山岩上，
遇着小蜜蜂：
"小蜜蜂，小蜜蜂！
你看见人种没有？"

"人种没看见，
葫芦见着了：
我去采花粉，
看见葫芦漂在河里面。
要是见了人，
我要请他吃蜜糖。"

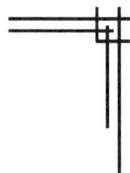

"In Spring wind blew three times,

And it rained three times.

I have not seen any human being.

If I met any,

I would use my dense leaves

To protect them from wind

And from rain."


Lord Gezi was pleased,

And he praised and honored this Buddhist pine:

"Buddhist pine, you are a good tree,

When I find a human being,

I will let them reproduce.

If people cut you down, you will reproduce a hundred new

ones."


Lord Gezi walked around mountain rocks,

Trying to find human beings.

He met a little bee:

"Little bee, little bee,

Have you ever seen any human being?"


"I have not seen any human being,

But I saw a big gourd.

When I was collecting pollen,

I saw a gourd floating on the river.

If I saw any human being,

I would share them with my sweet honey."

天神好喜欢，
封赠小蜜蜂：
"小蜜蜂，是好蜂，
等到人种找着了，
人烟旺起来，
让你挨着人家住。"

天神找人种，
河边河岸找，
遇着小柳树：
"小柳树，小柳树！
你看见人种没有？"

"人种没看见，
人声听见了：
我见一个大葫芦，
漂在水里面，
葫芦里面有人声。
用左手围也围不住，
用右手围也围不住，
葫芦淌走啦！"

天神好喜欢，
封赠小柳树：
"小柳树，是好树，
等到人种找到了，
人烟旺起来，
倒栽你倒活，
顺栽你顺活。"

Lord Gezi was pleased,

And he praised and honored this little bee:

"Little bee, you are a good bee,

When I find a human being,

I will let them reproduce.

You will live along with them."


Lord Gezi walked around riverbanks,

Trying to find human beings.

He met a little willow:

"Little willow, little willow,

Have you ever seen any human being?"


"I have not seen any human being,

But I have heard a human voice.

I saw a big gourd

Floating on the river,

A human voice came out of the gourd.

I failed to catch it with my left hand,

And I failed to stop it with my right hand.

The gourd floated away."


Lord Gezi was pleased,

And he praised and honored this willow,

"Little willow, you are a good tree,

When I find a human being,

I will let them reproduce.

No matter how they plant you,

You will survive."

天神找人种，
河头河尾找，
遇着老乌龟：
"老乌龟，老乌龟！
你看见人种没有？"

"大海中间葫芦里，
人的声音听得见，
你去叫叫看！"

天神好喜欢，
封赠老乌龟：
"老乌龟，心肠好，
敲下马蹄壳，
给你做房子，
房子随身带，
顺河有吃的。"

天神找人种，
来到大海边，
海边有个乌烟雀，
嗟嗟地叫着飞过来，
嗟嗟地叫着飞过去。
天神好生气：
"我找人种找不着，
心里好着急，
你这个乌烟雀，
还有什么喜欢的？"

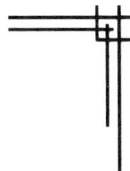

Lord Gezi walked around river sides,

Trying to find human beings.

He met an old turtle:

"Old turtle, old turtle,

Have you ever seen any human being?"


"There is a gourd in the sea,

And there is a human voice coming out of it.

You can go there to find it."


Lord Gezi was pleased,

And he praised and honored this turtle:

"Old turtle, you are very kind.

I will knock a horse hoof off

To make a shell for you to live in.

You can take it with you,

No matter where you swim and eat."


Lord Gezi walked to the seaside,

Trying to find human beings.

He saw a finch

Who was flying around

And singing "Jie-jie"①.

Lord Gezi was angry:

"I am worried that no human beings can be found.

You little finch,

What are you happy about?"

----

① Sounds made by a finch.

拉弓来射乌烟雀，
一箭射去射不着，
射中海边葫芦壳，
葫芦里头叫起来：
"已经五天没有人来打墙，
已经十天没有人来打墙，
今天哪个乱打我的墙？"

人种找到了，
天神好喜欢，
吩咐兄妹俩：
"世上人种子，
只剩你两个，
兄妹成亲传人烟。"

兄妹两个忙回答：
"我们两兄妹，
同胞父母生，
不能结成亲。"

说了很多，
比了很多。

兄妹在高山顶上滚石磨，
哥在这山滚上扇，
妹在那山滚下扇，
滚到山箐底，
上扇下扇合拢来。

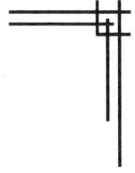

Lord Gezi took a bow to shoot it.

The arrow did not strike the finch,

But it stroke the gourd shell at the seaside.

A voice came out from inside:

"No one knocked the wall for five days,

No one knocked the wall for ten days,

Who is knocking the wall today?"

Lord Gezi was rejoiced

To find human beings at last.

He told the brother and sister:

"You two are the only two people in this world now,

You two will get married and reproduce human beings."

The brother and sister answered right away:

"We are brother and sister

Of the same parent,

And we can not get married."

Many words had been said,

Much explanation had been made.

The brother and sister rolled down a millstone from the

mountain top.

The brother rolled a bedstone,

And the sister rolled a runner stone.

They rolled each part down to the valley,

Bedstone and runner stone were then matched.

"你们两兄妹，
学磨成一家。"

"人是人，
磨是磨，
我们兄妹俩，
同胞父母生，
怎能学磨成一家。"

说了很多，
比了很多。
兄妹高山顶上滚筛子，
兄妹高山顶上滚簸箕。
哥在山阳滚筛子，
妹在山阴滚簸箕，
滚到山箐底，
筛子垒在簸箕上。

"你们两兄妹，
学筛子簸箕成一家。"

"筛子是筛子，
簸箕是簸箕，

"Brother and sister,

You should get married and make a family, just like that millstone."


"We are human beings,

Not millstones.

We are brother and sister of the same parent,

We are not like the millstones

And we can not get married."


Many words had been said,

Much explanation had been made.

The brother rolled down a Saizi① from the mountain top,

The sister rolled down a Boji② from the mountain top.

The brother rolled Saizi down from the sunny side,

And the sister rolled Boji down from the cloudy side.

They rolled each down to the valley,

Saizi and Boji were then matched.


"Brother and sister,

You should get married and make a family, just like that Saizi and Boji."


"We are human beings,

Not a Saizi or Boji.

_____

① Saizi is a kind of sieve, of the shape of a round shallow basket.
② Boji is a kind of round shallow basket.

我们兄妹俩，
同胞父母生，
怎能学它们成一家。"

说了很多，
比了很多。
天神指着说：
"箐底两只鸟，
一只是雄鸟，
一只是雌鸟，
雄的飞过来，
雌的飞过去，
雌鸟雄鸟在一起，
兄妹学鸟成一家。"

"人是人，
鸟是鸟，
不能学它成一家。"

说了很多，
比了很多。
天神指着说：
"这边一棵树，
那边一棵树，
一棵是公树，
一棵是母树。
东风吹来公树摇，
西风吹来母树摇，

We are brother and sister

Of the same parent,

And we cannot get married."


Many words had been said,

Much explanation had been made.

Lord Gezi pointed to two birds and said:

"There are two birds in the valley,

One is male,

The other is female.

One flies over,

The other flies over,

They two fly together.

You should get together, just like this pair of birds."


"We are human beings,

Not birds.

We can not get married."


Many words had been said,

Much explanation had been made.

Lord Gezi pointed to two trees and said:

"This is a tree,

That is a tree.

This tree is male,

That tree is female.

The male tree waves when the east wind blows,

The female tree waves when the west wind blows,

摇着摇着挨拢来，
挨拢成一家，
兄妹学树成一家。"

"人是人，
树是树，
不能学它成一家。"

说了很多，
比了很多。
兄妹二人来吆鸭，
兄妹二人来吆鹅。
哥在河这边，
妹在河那边。
哥哥吆公鸭，
妹妹吆母鸭；
哥哥吆公鹅，
妹妹吆母鹅。
公鸭母鸭成一家，
公鹅母鹅成一家。

"你们兄妹俩，
要学它们成一家。"

"人是人，
鸭是鸭，
鹅是鹅，
不能学它们成一家。"

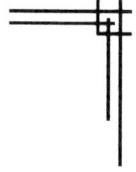

They get together while waving.
You two should get together,
Just like this pair of trees."

"We are human beings,
Not trees.
We can not get married."

Many words had been said,
Much explanation had been made.
The brother and sister called ducks,
The brother and sister called geese.
The brother called at one side of the river,
The sister called at the other side of the river.
The brother called male ducks,
The sister called female ducks.
The brother called male geese,
The sister called female geese.
Male and female ducks made families,
Male and female geese made families.

"Brother and sister,
You should get married and make a family, just like them."

"We are human beings,
Not ducks
Nor geese.
We can not get married."

"兄妹不愿结成亲,
世上怎能传人烟?"

"我们两兄妹,
同胞父母生,
成亲太害羞。
要传人烟有办法:
属狗那一天,
哥哥河头洗身子;
属猪那一天,
妹妹河尾捧水吃,
吃水来怀孕。"

一月吃一次,
吃了九个月。
妹妹怀孕了,
怀孕九个月,
生下一个怪葫芦。
哥哥不在家,
妹妹好害怕,
把葫芦丢在河里边。

天神知道了,

"If you two do not get married,

How can human beings reproduce?"

"We are brother and sister

Of the same parent,

And we are too shy to get married.

But to reproduce human beings, there is a way.

On a day of the dog①,

The brother washes his body in river's head.

On a day of the pig①,

The sister drinks the water from river's end.

She could get pregnant by drinking the water."

The sister drank the water once a month,

The sister drank the water for nine months,

The sister became pregnant.

After being pregnant for nine months,

She gave brith to a special gourd.

The brother was not at home,

And the sister was scared and all alone,

She discarded the gourd at the riverside.

After Lord Gezi learned this,

---

① It is related to the Chinese zodiac. The Chinese zodiac is a classification scheme that assigns an animal and its reputed attributes to each year in a repeating 12-year cycle. Here, the local people assign animals to each day as well.

急忙顺着河水找，
找到东洋大海边，
葫芦漂在水里面。

天神请来三对野猪，
拱开了海埂；
天神请来一对獭猫，
打了三个洞。
海埂拱开了，
洞子打开了，
海水还不落。
再请三对黄鳝，
请来钻海底。
海底钻通了，
水倒淌干了，
葫芦陷在泥浆里，
还是出不来。

天神请来三对兔鹰，
天神请来三对虾子。
兔鹰抓着葫芦飞，
虾子顶着葫芦走，
葫芦放在沙滩上，
金索银索拴葫芦，
金杆银杆抬葫芦，
抬到南京应天府①，

① 云南汉族都说祖先是由应天府迁来。这是后来的事被掺入诗中。

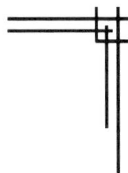

He immediately went look for the gourd along the river.

When Lord Gezi went to the east seaside,

He found the gourd floating there.

Lord Gezi asked three pairs of wild boars

To break the sea ridge.

Lord Gezi asked a pair of otters

To dig three holes.

The sea ridge was broken,

And the holes were dug,

But the seawater was still high.

Lord Gezi asked three pairs of eels

To dig the sea bottom.

The sea bottom was drilled through,

And the seawater dried up,

But the gourd was stuck in mud,

And could not come out.

Lord Gezi asked three pairs of eagles for help,

Lord Gezi asked three pairs of shrimps for help.

The eagles pulled the gourd out towards the sky,

The shrimps carried the gourd from its bottom.

The gourd was finally moved to the beach.

Gold and silver ropes were used to tie the gourd,

Gold and silver poles were used to lift the gourd,

The gourd was carried to Nanjing Yingtianfu①,

---

①　Yingtianfu, also called Nanjing, name of a region. It was one of the four capitals in the Song Dynasty. Han people in Yunnan Province believe that their ancestors were from Yingtianfu.

大坝柳树弯，
弯腰树下面。

葫芦找到了，
葫芦放好了，
天神用金锥开葫芦，
天神用银锥开葫芦。

戳开第一道，
出来是汉族。
汉族是老大，
住在坝子里，
耪田种庄稼，
读书学写字，
聪明本事大。

戳开第二道，
出来是傣族。
傣族办法好，
种出白棉花。

戳开第三道，
出来是彝家。
彝家住山里，
开地种庄稼。

And put under a crooked willow tree,

Nearby a dam.


The gourd was found,

The gourd was set.

With a gold awl and a silver awl,

Lord Gezi stabbed the gourd and opened it up.


With a first stab,

Lord Gezi brought Han people out from the gourd.

Han people became the favored ones.

They lived in the flatlands,

Plowing fields and planting crops,

Reading books and learning to write.

They were very clever and capable.


With a second stab,

Lord Gezi brought Dai people① out from the gourd.

Dai people had great ideas,

And became successful cotton farmers.


With a third stab,

Lord Gezi brought Yi people out from the gourd.

Yi people lived in the mountains,

Cultivating and planting crops.

---

　　① Han, Dai, Yi, Lisu, Miao, Zang, Bai, Hui are all ethnic groups.

戳开第四道，
出来是傈僳。
傈僳气力大，
出力背盐巴。

戳开第五道，
出来是苗家。
苗家人强壮，
住在高山上。

戳开第六道，
出来是藏族。
藏族很勇敢，
背弓打野兽。

戳开第七道，
出来是白族。
白族人很巧，
羊毛擀毡子，
纺线弹棉花。

戳开第八道，
出来是回族。
回族忌猪肉，
养牛吃牛肉。

戳开第九道，

With a fourth stab,

Lord Gezi brought Lisu people out from the gourd.

They had great physical strength,

Becoming salt carriers.


With a fifth stab,

Lord Gezi brought Miao people out from the gourd.

Miao people were very strong,

And they lived on the high mountains.


With a sixth stab,

Lord Gezi brought Zang people out from the gourd.

Zang people were very brave,

Carrying bows and hunting for beasts.


With a seventh stab,

Lord Gezi brought Bai people out from the gourd.

Bai people were handy,

And good at making wool felt,

Spinning thread and fluffing cotton.


With an eighth stab,

Lord Gezi brought Hui people out from the gourd.

Hui people did not eat pork,

And raised cattle for beef.


With a ninth stab,

出来是傣族①。
傣族盖寺庙,
念经信佛教。

出来九种族,
人烟兴旺了。

---

① 原文第二和第九都是"出来是傣族",今仍照原文。

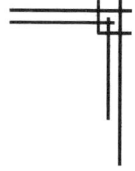

Lord Gezi brought Dai people① out from the gourd.

Dai people believed in Buddhism,

Building temples and reciting scriptures.


All nine ethnic groups were brought out,

And human beings proliferated.

---

① Based on the Chinese version, Dai people came out twice.

# 第二部　造　物

## 一、盖房子

哪个来盖房？
帕颇来盖房。
盖房没有树，
哪个撒树种？
帕颇撒树种。

东方山坡小姑娘，
树种草种是她撒。
帕颇向她要种子，
树种草种要来了。

什么是树王？
白菀树是树王，
先撒什么树？
先撒白菀树。

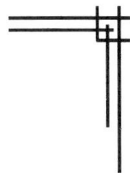

# Chapter Two　The Creation of Everything

## Section One　Housebuilding

Who would build houses?

Papo① would build houses.

There were no trees to build houses.

Who would sow tree seeds?

Papo would sow tree seeds.

There was a young lady living in the east hill,

She was responsible for sowing tree and grass seeds.

Papo asked her for some seeds,

And then there were trees and grass seeds.

What tree was the king of trees?

Baiwan tree was the king of trees.

What seeds should be sowed first?

Baiwan② seeds should be sowed first.

---

① Papo, name of a person.

② Baiwan is one species of Turczaninowia in the composite family. It's a common traditional Chinese medicine.

高山顶顶上，
撒了白菀树；
高山梁子上，
撒了青松和赤松；
高山箐沟里，
撒上青香树。

坝区山腰上，
撒了罗汉松，
撒了桂皮树，
撒了梧桐树，
撒了梨树桃树，
撒了花红树，
撒了核桃树，
撒了樱桃树。

坝区山坡上，
撒了橄榄树；
坝区岩顶上，
撒下鸡嗉子树。
河头①两岸上，
撒了水冬瓜树；

---

① 河头：即河的上游，彝族人把河的上游、中游、下游常说为
河头、河中、河尾。

On top of high mountains,

Papo sowed Baiwan seeds.

On ridges of high mountains,

Papo sowed green pine and red pine seeds.

On valley of high mountains,

Papo sowed Qingxiang tree① seeds.


On hill sides in the flatlands,

Papo sowed Buddhist pine seeds,

Cassia seeds,

Phoenix tree seeds,

Pear tree seeds and peach tree seeds,

Huahong tree② seeds,

Walnut tree seeds,

Cherry tree seeds.


On the hill slopes in the flatlands,

Papo sowed olive tree seeds.

On rock tops in the flatlands,

Papo sowed Jisuozi tree③ seeds.

On banks of river upstream,

Papo sowed Shuidonggua④ seeds.

---

① Qingxiang tree is one species of the Pistacia in the cashew family.

② Huahong tree is one species of the Malus in the rose family. In Latin, it's called Malus asiatica Nakai.

③ Jisuozi tree is one species of the Cornus. In Latin, it's called Dendrobenthamia capitate.

④ Shuidonggua is one species of Alnus in the birch family. In Latin, it's called Alnus cremastogyne. It's a common traditional Chinese medicine.

河边两岸上，
撒了杨柳树，
撒了麻栎树，
撒了锥栗树。

野香樟树撒了三岭，
马缨花树撒了三岭，
白皮松树撒了三凹，
橡树栗树撒了三坡，
橡树栗树撒了三箐。
树种撒下了，
河边两岸都撒遍，
山山箐箐都撒到。

什么是草王？
芦苇是草王。
先撒什么草籽？

先撒芦苇草籽。
高山梁子上，
撒下芦苇草，
撒下野芭籽；

Along the river banks,

Papo sowed willow seeds,

Cedar seeds,

And chestnut seeds.


Camphor tree seeds were scattered over mountain ridges,

Mayinghua tree① seeds were sowed over mountain ridges,

White pine seeds were scattered over mountain basins,

Oak seeds and chestnut seeds were sowed over mountain
slopes,

Oak seeds and chestnut seeds were scattered over mountain
valleys.

Papo sowed all those tree seeds,

All along the riverbanks,

All over the mountains.


What grass was the king of grass?

Reed was the king of grass.

What seeds should be sowed first?


Reed seeds should be sowed first.

On ridges of high mountains,

Papo sowed reed seeds

And wild plantain seeds.

---

① Mayinghua is one species of Albizzia in the pea family. In Latin,
it's called Albizia julibrissin. It's a common traditional Chinese medicine.

高山箐底下，
撒下鸡菜籽，
撒下菱角草，
撒下蕨菜籽，
撒下兔子草。

坝区山坡上，
撒了山头草；
坝区岩子上，
撒了甘草籽，
撒了山草籽；
坝区地边上，
撒了酸草籽；
坝区河边上，
撒了红白厚皮草，
撒了岩草籽。
河边两岸上，
撒了山野菜；
沟边两岸上，
撒了喂猪草；
房前屋后头，
撒了黄麻籽。

On valley of high mountains,

Papo sowed Jicai① seeds,

Water chestnut seeds,

Fiddlehead seeds,

And water spinach seeds.


On the hill slopes in the flatlands,

Papo sowed hilltop grass seeds.

Around rocks in the flatlands,

Papo sowed glycyrrhiza seeds

And hillgrass seeds.

On lands in the flatlands,

Papo sowed Suancao② seeds.

Along riverbanks in the flatlands,

Papo sowed red and white grass seeds

And rockweed seeds.

Along the riverbanks,

Papo sowed hill potherb seeds.

Along the valleys,

Papo sowed pigweed seeds.

Around the houses,

Papo sowed Huangma③ seeds.

---

① Jicai is one species of Capsella in the mustard family. In English, it is called Shepherdspurse Herb.

② Suancao is one species of Oxalis. In Latin, it's called Oxalis corniculata L.

③ Huangma is one species of tiliaceae. In Latin, it's called Corchorus capsularis L.

草种撒下了，
平坝地区上，
山岩河边上，
高山箐底下，
处处都撒遍，
样样都撒了。


帕颇有九个儿子，
九个儿子来养树；
帕颇有七个姑娘，
七姊妹来养草。
过了三十七天后，
树芽迎风摆，
草芽迎风摇。
三轮三十七，
四轮四十九，
五轮六十一，
六轮七十三，
七轮八十四，
八轮九十五，
树长大了，
草长大了。
长满三山岭，
长满偏坡地。


帕颇的九个儿子，
把树养大了；
帕颇的七个姑娘，

Grass seeds were planted

All over flatlands,

All over the rocks, mountains and valleys,

All along the riverbanks.

Grass seeds were sowed everywhere.

Every kind of seeds were planted.


Papo had nine sons,

They would cultivate trees.

Papo had seven daughters,

They would cultivate grass.

After thirty-seven days,

There were tree buds waving in wind,

There were grass sprouts dancing in wind.

Three rounds were thirty-seven days,

Four rounds were forty-nine days,

Five rounds were sixty-one days,

Six rounds were seventy-three days,

Seven rounds were eighty-four days,

Eight rounds were ninety-five days.

Trees had grown tall,

Grass had grown tall.

They had covered all hills,

They had covered all lands.


Papo's nine sons

Had grown trees.

Papo's seven daughters

把草养大了。
天上九兄弟，
想盖九间房。
什么地方盖房子？
树林当中盖了九间房。

白樱桃树盖了三间房，
人间九种族，
傣族来住房。
坝区山腰上，
罗汉松树盖了三间房，
哪个来住房？
回族来住房。

高山梁子上，
青松赤松盖了三间房，
哪个来住房？
彝族来住房。

坝区平坝上，
青香树盖了三间房，
哪个来住房？
汉族来住房。

高山梁子上，
洋皮松树盖了三间房，
哪个来住房？
打柴打猎的人来住房。

Had grown grass.

These nine brothers

Wanted to build nine houses.

Where did they build houses?

They built houses among woods.


White cherry trees were used to build three houses.

There were nine ethnic groups in the human world.

Dai people would live there.

On hill sides in the flatlands,

Buddhist pines were used to build three houses.

Who would live in these houses?

Hui people would live in these houses.


On ridges of high mountains,

Green pines and red pines were used to build three houses.

Who would live in these houses?

Yi people would live in these houses.


On flatlands,

Qingxiang trees were used to build three houses.

Who would live in these houses?

Han people would live in these houses.


On ridges of high mountains,

Pines were used to build three houses.

Who would live in these houses?

Hunters and woodmen would live in these houses.

野白松树来盖房，
哪个来住房？
擀毡子的人来住房。

野香樟树盖了三间房，
哪个来住房？
放羊的人来住房。

河边两岸盖了三间房，
哪个来住房？
放牛的人来住房。

盖也盖好了，
住的住好了，
天王地王都喜欢。

什么是兽王？
兔子是兽王。
刺树盖起三间房，
兔子来住房。

高山梁子上，
盖起三间石头房，
什么来住房？
老虎来住房。

坝区山腰上，
盖起三间土平房，

Wild pines were used to build houses.

Who would live in these houses?

Felt makers would live in these houses.


Camphor trees were used to build houses.

Who would live in these houses?

Sheepherders would live in these houses.


Three houses were built along riverbanks.

Who would live in these houses?

Cowherds would live in these houses.


Houses were built,

People settled down.

Lords in heaven and lords on earth were all delighted.


What animal was the king of animals?

Rabbit was the king of animals.

Thorn trees were used to build three houses,

Rabbits would live in these houses.


On ridges of high mountains,

Three stone houses were built.

Who would live in these houses?

Tigers would live in these houses.


On hill sides in the flatlands,

Three clay cottages were built.

什么来住房？
豹子来住房。

高山梁子上，
橡树盖起三间房，
什么来住房？
老熊来住房。

高山顶顶上，
刺杆盖起三间房，
什么来住房？
豺狼来住房。

坝区河边上，
樱桃树木来盖房，
什么来住房？
麂子来住房。

石岩下面盖起三间房，
什么来住房？
马鹿来住房。

山中石岩上，
香樟树盖起三间房，
什么来住房？
岩羊来住房。

不够又盖三间房，

Who would live in these houses?

Leopards would live in these houses.


On ridges of high mountains,

Oaks were used to build three houses,

Who would live in these houses?

Old bears would live in these houses.


On top of high mountains,

Thistles were used to build three houses.

Who would live in these houses?

Jackals would live in these houses.


Along riverbanks in the flatlands,

Cherries were used to build houses.

Who would live in these houses?

Muntjacs would live in these houses.


Three houses were built under mountain rocks.

Who would live in these houses?

Elks would live in these houses.


On mountains rocks,

Camphor trees were used to build three houses.

Who would live in these houses?

Blue sheep would live in these houses.


Still there were not enough houses,

盖在岩洞里，
什么来住房？
野牛来住房。

坝区河岸上，
盖起三间房，
什么来住房？
豪猪来住房。

高山梁子上，
盖起三间土洞房，
什么来住房？
穿山甲来住房。

河里石头盖起三间房。
什么来住房？
水獭来住房。

兽类的房子盖好了，
兽类有了房子住。

什么是鸟王？
凤凰是鸟王。
坝区山腰上，
梧桐树盖起三间房，
凤凰来住房。

坝区岩子上，

So three more houses were built in caves.

Who would live in these houses?

Bison would live in these houses.


Along riverbanks in the flatlands,

Three houses were built.

Who would live in these houses?

Porcupines would live in these houses.


On ridges of high mountains,

Three cave houses were built.

Who would live in these houses?

Pangolins would live in these houses.


River stone were used to build three houses.

Who would live in these houses?

Otters would live in these houses.


Houses were built,

Animals settled down.


What bird was the king of birds?

Phoenix was the king of birds.

On hill sides in the flatlands,

Phoenix trees were used to build three houses,

Phoenix would live in these houses.


On rocks in the flatlands,

盖起三间房，
什么来住房？
大雁来住房。

林中落叶盖起三间房，
什么来住房？
岩鸡来住房。

半山橡子林中间，
刺枝盖起三间房，
什么来住房？
老鹰来住房。

高山箐沟里，
橡子树叶盖起三间房，
什么来住房？
箐鸡野鸡来住房。

坝区山腰上，
樱桃树枝来盖房，
什么来住房？
斑鸠来住房。

河边两岸上，
核桃树盖起三间房，
什么来住房？
老鸹喜鹊来住房。

Three houses were built.

Who would live in these houses?

Wild geese would live in these houses.


Fallen leaves in the woods were used to build three houses.

Who would live in these houses?

Wild roosters would live in these houses.


In oak woods on a mountainside,

Thorns were used to build three houses.

Who would live in these houses?

Eagles would live in these houses.


On valley of high mountains,

Oak leaves were used to build three houses.

Who would live in these houses?

Pheasants would live in these houses.


On hill sides in the flatlands,

Cherry brunches were used to build houses.

Who would live in these houses?

Turtledoves would live in these houses.


Along the riverbanks,

Walnut trees were used to build three houses.

Who would live in these houses?

Crows and magpies would live in these houses.

林中落叶盖起三间房，
什么来住房？
杂鸟来住房。

高山梁子上，
青松盖起三间房，
什么来住房？
猫头鹰来住房。

坝区山腰上，
用土舂起三间房，
什么来住房？
鹦虎雀子来住房。

再用落叶盖起三间房，
什么来住房？
鹦哥来住房。

山中岩子上，
花红树木盖起三间房，
什么来住房？
小燕子来住房。

不够再来盖，
拿草盖起三间房，
什么来住房？
蚂蚱来住房。

Fallen leaves in the woods were used to build three houses.

Who would live in these houses?

Birds would live in these houses.

On ridges of high mountains,

Green pines were used to build three houses.

Who would live in these houses?

Owls would live in these houses.

On hill sides in the flatlands,

Soil was used to build three houses.

Who would live in these houses?

Sparrows would live in these houses.

Fallen leaves in the woods were used to build three houses.

Who would live in these houses?

Parrots would live in these houses.

On mountain rocks,

Huahong trees were used to build three houses.

Who would live in these houses?

Little swallows would live in these houses.

Still there were not enough houses,

So grass was used to build three more houses.

Who would live in these houses?

Grasshoppers would live in these houses.

河里盖了三间石头房，
什么来住房？
石蚌来住房。

江底盖了三间石头房，
什么来住房？
鲤鱼来住房。

各样房子都盖齐，
各样房子都盖好，
鸟兽虫鱼有房住。

盖也盖好了，
住的住好了，
天王地王都喜欢。

## 二、狩猎和畜牧

上山打猎去，
上山撵麂子去。
撵麂子要有猎狗，
撵麂子要用麻索，
撵麂子要用猎网。
哪里有猎狗？
哪里出麻索？
哪里出猎网？

Three stone houses were built in rivers.

Who would live in these houses?

Clams would live in these houses.


Three stone houses were built under rivers.

Who would live in these houses?

Carps would live in these houses.


Houses were built,

Houses were built well.

Animals, birds and insects settled down.


Houses were built,

People settled down.

Lords in heaven and lords on earth were all delighted.

# Section Two   Hunting and Livestock-raising

People should hunt in the hills,

People should hunt muntjacs in the hills.

A hound was needed to hunt muntjacs,

A hemp rope was needed to hunt muntjacs,

A hunting net was needed to hunt muntjacs.

Where would people get hounds?

Where would people get hemp ropes?

Where would people get hunting nets?

大理苍山黄石头，
黄石头变黄狗，
它就是猎狗。

傈僳族会撒麻，
傈僳族会种麻，
傈僳族会剥麻，
找傈僳族去。
找到山腰上，
到了傈僳族住的地方。

撒麻的人有了，
种麻的人有了，
剥麻的人有了，
还没有人搓麻索，
还没有人结猎网。

格滋天神说：
"没有搓麻索的人不要着急，
没有结猎网的人不要心焦。
去找特勒么的女人，
她会搓麻索，
她会结猎网。"

There were yellow stones in Mount Cangshan in Dali①,

Yellow stones could transform into yellow dogs,

They could become hounds.


Lisu people knew how to sow hemp seeds,

Lisu people knew how to grow hemp,

Lisu people knew how to get hemp fibers.

Lisu people should be found.

People went to the mountainsides,

And found Lisu people who lived there.


Then there were people to sow hemp seeds,

There were people to grow hemp,

There were people to get hemp fibers,

But there were no people to make hemp ropes,

And there were no people to weave hunting nets.


Lord Gezi said,

"No worry about who to make hemp ropes,

No worry about who to weave hunting nets.

Go and find the wife of Teleme②,

She knows how to make hemp ropes,

She knows how to weave hunting nets."

---

① Mount Cangshan is a well-known mountain located in Dali region in Yunnan Province.

② There are no resources for more information about Teleme. It might be a name of a region or a name of a person. Here the translator takes it as a name of a person.

特勒么的女人，
一天能搓三丈，
三天能搓九丈；
一天能结三丈，
三天能结九丈。
越搓越喜欢，
越结越高兴。
麻索越搓越长，
猎网越结越好。

猎狗找到了，
麻索搓成了，
猎网也结好了。
吆着猎狗，
拿着麻索，
拿着猎网，
上山撵麂子。

公麂子出在茶山，
母麂子出在东洋大海石岩边。
有麂子的地方知道了，
还没有撵麂子的人。
天神的儿子，
开天的那五兄弟，
大儿子阿赌会撵山，
叫他撵麂子去。

114

The wife of Teleme

Could spin three Zhang of rope in one day,

She could spin nine Zhang of rope in three days.

She could tie three Zhang of rope in one day,

She could tie nine Zhang of rope in three days.

She was exhilarated when spinning ropes,

She was excited when tying ropes.

Hemp ropes were made longer and longer,

Hunting nets were made better and better.


Hounds were found,

Hemp ropes were made,

Hunting nets were woven.

With hounds,

Hemp ropes,

And hunting nets,

People were ready to go hunting muntjacs in the hills.


Male muntjacs were in Mount Tea,

Female muntjacs were among mountain rocks by Eastern Ocean.

Then it was known where people would hunt muntjacs,

But it was not certain who would hunt muntjacs.

Gambling was one of the sons of Lord Gezi,

He was one of the five brothers who made the sky.

Gambling knew how to hunt,

He would go hunting muntjacs.

阿赌领着猎狗，
拿着麻索，
拿着猎网，
到茶山去撵公麂子，
到东洋大海去撵母麂子。
大儿子阿赌，
到了茶山上，
走进大树林，
放出恶猎狗，
一只麂子也没有。

大儿子阿赌，
到了东洋大海边，
走进小树林，
放出恶猎狗，
撵出来三四只麂子。

麂子跑出来，
阿赌拼命追，
从山头到山脚，
从河头到河尾，
追过一山又一山，
追过一林又一林，
追到大河边。

河水弯又弯，
河水清又清，
河水深，

116

Gambling led his hound,

He took his hemp rope

And hunting net,

He went to Mount Tea to hunt male muntjacs,

He went to Eastern Ocean to hunt female muntjacs.

Gambling, the Number One son of Lord Gezi,

Went to Mount Tea,

He walked into the woods,

He unleashed his fierce hound,

But found no muntjacs.


Gambling, the Number One son of Lord Gezi,

Went near Eastern Ocean,

He walked into the woods,

He unleashed his fierce hound,

And found several muntjacs.


Muntjacs ran away,

Gambling chased after them.

From hilltop to its foot,

From river's head to its end,

From one hill to another,

From one woods to another,

And finally Gambling came to a big river.


The river was curvy,

The river was clear,

The water was deep,

波浪滚，
麂子顺着小路跑，
麂子顺着小路逃。
河边小路旁，
长满了藤窝，
藤子牵藤子。
绊住麂子脚，
绊是绊住了，
杀是杀不着，
捞起海里的大石头，
甩进藤窝打麂子，
麂子打死了，
麂子皮拿来做衣裳，
麂子肉分给大家吃。

打的野物不够吃，
要去耪田种地收五谷。
耪田没有牛，
种地没有牛，
要去找牛啦。

牛从哪里来？
大理苍山上，
露水下下来，
红露水变成红牛，
黄露水变成黄牛，
黑露水变成黑牛。
哪个先看见？

The stream was rushy.

Muntjacs ran along a track,

Muntjacs ran away along the track.

There were vine plants

Spreading all over on the sides of the track.

Vine plants were stumbling,

And tripped muntjacs' feet.

Muntjacs were tripped now,

But Gambling could not reach them.

Gambling got a big stone from sea,

And threw it towards the muntjacs.

Muntjacs were killed.

Their skin was taken to make clothes,

And their flesh was taken to make dishes.


The prey was not enough for food,

People needed to plow fields and grow crops.

There were no cattle to pull a plow,

There were no cattle to help people.

Ah! People would go and find cattle.


How did the cattle come into being?

On Mount Cangshan in Dali,

There was dew dropping down.

Red dew transformed into red cattle,

Yellow dew transformed into yellow cattle,

Black dew transformed into black cattle.

Who found the cattle first?

葫芦蜂爱露水,
它去采露水,
它先看见牛。

哪个把牛找回来?
特勒么的女人,
左手拿盐巴,
右手拿春草,
把牛哄住了。
树藤来拴牛,
把牛牵回来。

牛拴回来啦,
牛已经有啦!
没有放牛的地方,
什么地方好放牛?
高山箐沟里,
河边两岸青草地,
那是放牛的好地方。

有了牛,
还没有猪,
什么地方有猪?
南京应天府,
大坝柳树弯,
是出猪的地方。

猪从哪里来?

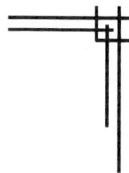

Bees loved dew,

While they collected dew,

They found the cattle first.

Who would bring the cattle back?

The wife of Teleme would.

She knew how to satisfy the cattle

With salt in her left hand

And spring grass in her right hand.

She led the cattle with tree vines,

She brought the cattle back.

Ah! The cattle were brought back.

Ah! There were cattle now.

Where would people herd cattle?

Where was a good place to herd cattle?

In the valley of high mountains,

There was grassland along the riverbanks.

It was perfect to herd cattle there.

There were cattle now,

But there were no pigs yet.

Where would people get pigs?

In Nanjing Yingtianfu,

There was a crooked willow tree nearby a dam,

There were pigs there.

How did the pig come into being?

白云彩变白露，
黑云彩变黑露，
天上下白露，
天上下黑露
露水会扎地，
白露扎出白石头，
黑露扎出黑石头。
天神下凡来，
打烂白石头，
白猪钻出来；
打烂黑石头，
黑猪钻出来。

有了白猪，
有了黑猪，
还没有羊。
什么地方有羊？
南京应天府，
大坝柳树弯，
是出羊的地方。

羊从哪里来？
大理苍山有三个松树桩，
松树桩里有三条白虫，
白虫变成白绵羊；
大理苍山有三个铁栗木树桩，
铁栗木树桩里有三条黑虫，
黑虫变成黑山羊。

122

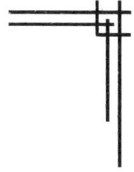

White clouds transformed into white dew,

Black clouds transformed into black dew.

White dew dropped from the sky,

Black dew dropped from the sky.

When dew dropped to the ground,

White dew transformed into white stones,

Black dew transformed into black stones.

A lord in heaven came down to help,

He broke white stones,

And white pigs came out.

He broke black stones,

And black pigs came out.


There were white pigs now,

There were black pigs now,

But there were no sheep yet.

Where would people get sheep?

In Nanjing Yingtianfu,

There was a crooked willow tree nearby a dam,

There were sheep there.


How did sheep come into being?

There were three pine stumps on Mount Cangshan in Dali,

There were three white worms in those pine stumps,

These white worms transformed into white sheep.

There were three chestnut stumps on Mount Cangshan in

Dali,

There were three black worms in those chestnut stumps,

These black worms transformed into black goats.

有了猪，
有了羊，
还没有放猪的人，
还没有放羊的人。
什么人会放猪？
什么人会放羊？
汉族会放猪，
彝族会放羊。

放猪的人有了，
放羊的人有了，
还没有吆猪棍，
还没有赶羊鞭。
拿什么做吆猪棍？
拿什么做赶羊鞭？
没有吆猪棍不要怕，
没有赶羊鞭不要怕。
山上有黄竹，
砍节黄竹能吆猪，
砍节黄竹能赶羊。

放猪的女人，
放羊的男人，
下雨天气冷，
没有蓑衣和笠帽。
没有蓑衣不要怕，
没有笠帽不要怕。
山上有茅草，

There were pigs now,

There were sheep now,

But there were no people to herd pigs,

And there were no people to herd sheep.

Who knew how to herd pigs?

Who knew how to herd sheep?

Han people knew how to herd pigs,

Yi people knew how to herd sheep.


Now there were people to herd pigs,

Now there were people to herd sheep,

But there were no rods to herd pigs,

And there were no whips to herd sheep.

What should people use as rods to herd pigs?

What should people use as whips to herd sheep?

No worry about having no rods,

No worry about having no whips.

There was yellow bamboo on the mountains,

Bamboo branches could be used as rods,

Bamboo twigs could be used as whips.


In those cold rainy days,

Women who herded pigs,

Men who herded sheep,

had no straw raincoats

Or bamboo hats.

No worry about having no straw raincoats,

No worry about having no bamboo hats.

梅葛 Meige

割回茅草连蓑衣；
山上有篾子，
编好篾子，
铺上棕叶子，
篾帽做好了。
身上穿蓑衣，
风吹不进，
雨淋不湿。
头上戴笠帽，
风吹不着，
雨淋不着。

放猪的女人，
放羊的男人，
没有鞋子穿，
爬山脚要疼。
山上有茅草，
割来打草鞋，
穿上新草鞋，
爬山脚不疼。

什么都有了，
还没有放猪的地方，
还没有放羊的地方。
什么地方好放猪？
什么地方好放羊？
河岸长满爬根草，
池边尽是烂泥塘，

126

There were straws grown on the mountains,

Straws would be used to make straw raincoats.

There were bamboo strips grown on mountains,

Bamboo strips would be woven into hats,

Hats would be covered with palm leaves.

Then bamboo hats were created.

Wearing straw raincoats.

Men and women were protected from wind

And rain.

Wearing bamboo hats,

Men and women were protected from wind

And rain.


Women who herded pigs

And men who herded sheep

Had no shoes to wear.

Their feet got hurt while climbing mountains.

There were straws on mountains,

Straws could be used to make sandals.

Wearing new straw sandals,

Men and women would not hurt their feet anymore.


People then had everything,

But there were no places to herd pigs,

But there were no places to herd sheep.

Where would people herd pigs?

Where would people herd sheep?

There was grass grown all over by the river,

There were muddy ponds all over by the river.

那是放猪的好地方；
有三条大箐沟，
长满了藤窝，
有三匹山岭，
长满了水马松，
那是放羊的好地方。

放猪的地方有了，
放羊的地方有了，
在河边放猪，
在山上放羊，
放猪放得好，
放羊放得好，
猪长得肥，
羊长得壮。

山野放猪没有伴，
山野放羊没有伴；
放猪没有伴不要怕，
放羊没有伴不要怕。
四川人的三个儿子会砍竹竿，
四川人的三个儿子会做篾活，
竹头拿来做葫芦笙，
竹中间拿来做笛子，
竹根拿来做响篾。

They were perfect places to herd pigs.

There were three valleys

Where vine plants spread all over,

There were three hill ridges

Where water pines grew all over.

They were perfect places to herd sheep.


Then there were places to herd pigs,

And places to herd sheep.

People herded pigs by the river,

They herded sheep on the hills.

People herded pigs well,

They herded sheep well.

Pigs grew fat,

Sheep grew strong.


People had no companions while herding pigs,

They had no companions while herding sheep.

No worry about having no companions while herding pigs,

No worry about having no companions while herding sheep.

Three sons of Sichuan people① could cut bamboo,

Three sons of Sichuan people could weave bamboo strips.

Bamboo head could be used to make Hulusheng②,

Bamboo body could be used to make flute,

Bamboo root could be used to make Xiangmie③.

①    Sichuan is a province in Southwestern China.

②    Hulusheng: a Chinese traditional instrument.

③    Xiangmie is a kind of mouth organ which is made from bamboo.
This instrument is popular among ethnic groups in Yunnan Province.

放猪放羊,
葫芦笙做伴;
放猪放羊,
笛子做伴;
放猪放羊,
响篾做伴。

放猪的女人有芦笙,
放羊的男人有芦笙;
放猪的女人有笛子,
放羊的男人有笛子;
放猪的女人有响篾,
放羊的男人有响篾。

吹着芦笙,
吹着笛子,
弹起响篾。
山头吹一调,
山尾弹一曲,
欢乐得起来,
唱得起来,
放猪的女人喜欢,
放羊的男人喜欢。

# 三、农事

坎上种包谷,
坎下种荞子,

While herding pigs and sheep,

People had Hulusheng as their companion.

While herding pigs and sheep,

People had flute as their companion.

While herding pigs and sheep,

People had Xiangmie as their companion.

Women who herded pigs had Hulusheng,

Men who herded sheep had Hulusheng.

Women who herded pigs had flutes,

Men who herded sheep had flutes.

Women who herded pigs had Xiangmie,

Men who herded sheep had Xiangmie.

People played Hulusheng,

They played flute,

They played Xiangmie.

People sang together,

On hilltop,

On hillfoot.

People entertained themselves.

Women who herded pigs enjoyed it,

Men who herded sheep enjoyed it.

## Section Three   Agriculture

People planted corn on upper field ridges,

People planted buckwheat on lower field ridges.

水冬瓜树下的荞子好，
锥栗树下的荞子好，
有松树的坡地，
甜荞长得好。

山坡杂树多，
根多不好耪庄稼，
人类拿刀子，
要把树砍完。
兔子争了先，
先去砍树枝，
砍也砍不倒。
豺狼去砍枝，
还是砍不倒。
老虎去砍枝，
还是砍不倒。
麂子去砍枝，
还是砍不倒。
麻雀去砍枝，
还是砍不倒。
大雁又来砍，
还是砍不倒。
老鸹又来砍，
还是砍不倒。
野鸡也来砍，
还是砍不倒。
竹鸡也来砍，
还是砍不倒。

Buckwheat grew well under Shuidonggua trees,

Buckwheat grew well under Chestnut trees.

Sweet buckwheat grew well

On slopes where there were pines.


There were many unwanted trees on the hill slopes.

The myriad roots of these trees were not good for plowing.

People intended to use axes

To cut these trees down.

Rabbits came first,

They tried to cut branches first,

But failed.

Jackals tried to cut branches,

But failed.

Tigers tried to cut branches,

But failed.

Muntjacs tried to cut branches,

But failed.

Sparrows tried to cut branches,

But failed.

Wild geese tried to cut branches,

But failed.

Crows tried to cut branches,

But failed.

Pheasants tried to cut branches,

But failed.

Partridge tried to cut branches,

But failed.

鹦哥也来砍，
还是砍不倒。
乌鸦也来砍，
还是砍不倒。
百兽都砍了，
百兽砍不倒。
百鸟都砍了，
百鸟砍不倒。

人来砍杂树，
先把刀磨好，
拿刀来砍枝，
几刀便砍倒！
地王就决定：
人类耢庄稼。

五月砍到六月来，
六月砍到七月来，
七月砍到八月来，
八月砍到九月来。
山山箐箐，
河头河尾，
杂树全都砍光了。

十月晒一月，
冬月接着晒；
冬月晒一月，
晒到腊月尾。

Parrots tried to cut branches,
But failed.
Ravens tried to cut branches,
But failed.
All animals had a try,
But failed.
All birds had a try,
But failed.

Then it was people's turn.
They sharpened an axe first,
And cut branches with it.
They succeeded with their axes.
Lord Gezi thus decided:
People would plow fields.

People started to cut trees from May to June,
From June to July,
From July to August,
From August to September.
On all hills and valleys,
Along riverbanks,
All unwanted trees were cut down.

People let fields rest under the sun in October,
And rest under the sun in November,
And rest under the sun in December.
People let fields rest for a whole winter.

过了旧历年，
正月初一那一天，
房前屋后雀鸟叫，
梁下雀鸟来做窝，
节令分出来了，
要忙庄稼活路了。

二月二十七，
布谷鸟叫起来，
石蚌叫起来，
要放火烧荞地了。
野兽来烧火，
还是烧不着。
鸟类来烧火，
还是烧不着。
最后来决定：
还是人来烧。

属牛日来烧，
恐怕烧着牛。
属虎日来烧，
恐怕烧着虎。

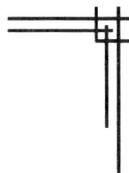

On the first day of January

Of the Lunar New Year,

Birds sang around their houses,

Birds made new nests on roof beams.

Then it was time to plow.

People were ready for growing crops.


On February the twenty-seventh,

Cuckoos started to sing,

Clams started to sing,

It was time to set fire to buckwheat fields.

Beasts tried to set fire,

But failed.

Birds tried to set fire,

But failed.

Lord Gezi thus decided:

People would set fire.


People would not set fire on a day of the ox①,

They were afraid of burning oxes.

People would not set fire on a day of the tiger,

They were afraid of burning tigers.

---

① It is related to the Chinese Zodiac, known as Sheng Xiao. Chinese Zodiac is based on a twelve-year cycle, each year in that cycle related to an animal sign. These signs in order are the rat, ox, tiger, rabbit, dragon, snake, horse, sheep, monkey, rooster, dog and pig. It is calculated according to Chinese lunar calendar. Here in the text, each day is related to an animal sign as well.

属兔日来烧，
恐怕烧着兔。
属龙日来烧，
恐怕烧着龙。
属蛇日来烧，
恐怕烧着蛇。
属马日来烧，
恐怕烧着马。
属羊日来烧，
恐怕烧着羊。
属猴日来烧，
恐怕烧着猴。
属鸡日来烧，
恐怕烧着鸡。
属狗日来烧，
恐怕烧着狗。
属猪日来烧，
恐怕烧着猪。
最后商量好，
选在属鼠日。
老鼠会打洞，
不会被火烧。

从此火着了，
荒地烧起来。
火烟冲上天，
火烟冲过江，
火焰挡不住，

People would not set fire on a day of the rabbit,

They were afraid of burning rabbits.

People would not set fire on a day of the dragon,

They were afraid of burning dragons.

People would not set fire on a day of the snake,

They were afraid of burning snakes.

People would not set fire on a day of the horse,

They were afraid of burning horses.

People would not set fire on a day of the sheep,

They were afraid of burning sheep.

People would not set fire on a day of the monkey,

They were afraid of burning monkeys.

People would not set fire on a day of the rooster,

They were afraid of burning roosters.

People would not set fire on a day of the dog,

They were afraid of burning dogs.

People would not set fire on a day of the pig,

They were afraid of burning pigs.

People finally decided

To set fire on a day of the rat,

Because rats could dig holes

And would not get burnt.


People set fire,

Buckwheat field caught fire.

With flames roaring up into the sky,

With flames shooting across the river,

Flames got out of control,

仓房烧毁了，
籽种烧光了，
荞种没有了。
亏得天上小麻雀，
四面八方拣荞种，
荞种拣来了。
三月二十日，
开地撒荞子。

属龙日来撒，
庄稼像龙一样旺！
属虎日来撒，
庄稼像虎一样好。

哪个来犁地？
男人来犁地。
哪个来撒种？
妇女来撒种。
撒好八十八座梁，
撒好七十七匹坡。
过了十三天，
庄稼长得肥又旺；
三十七天后，
庄稼长得更好了。

薅草节令到，
铲草节令到。
这回七姊妹，

And burned all warehouses,

all seeds,

And all buckwheat seeds.

Luckily there were little sparrows,

Helping to pick buckwheat seeds from far and near.

Enough buckwheat seeds were collected.

On March the twentieth,

People started to plow fields and sow buckwheat seeds.


People worked on days of the dragon,

So that crops would grow as strong as dragons.

People worked on days of the tiger,

So that crops would grow as strong as tigers.


Who would plow the fields?

Men would plow the fields.

Who would sow seeds?

Women would sow seeds.

They sowed seeds all over eighty-eight hill ridges,

They sowed seeds all over seventy-seven hillslopes.

Thirteen days passed,

Crops grew well and strong.

Thirty-seven days passed,

Crops grew better and stronger.


Then it was time to weed the fields,

Then it was time to remove the weeds.

The seven sisters took turns to work on it,

一人薅一天。
到了九月土黄天，
庄稼薅好了。

箐底到山顶，
山凹到平坝，
没有不种庄稼的地方，
到处的庄稼都薅好了。
庄稼长得好，
玉米长得像马尾，
荞子长得像葡萄。
兽类去看，
看了很佩服；
鸟类也去看，
看了很佩服。
从此就是人类薅庄稼。

人来薅庄稼，
要按节令薅。
把年月日分出来，
把四季分出来，
才好薅庄稼。
哪个来分年月日？
天神来分年月日。
一年十个月，
一月四十天①

———————————

① 传说最早的时候，人类是这样错分年月日的。

Everyone worked for one day.

When September came,

Crops were fully grown.


From mountain tops to valleys,

From mountain basins to flatlands,

People grew crops everywhere,

Crops were fully grown everywhere.

Crops grew well and strong,

Corn was like horsetails,

Buckwheat was like grapes.

After seeing this,

Beasts were impressed.

After seeing this,

Birds were impressed.

From that time on, it was human beings who grew crops.


People should plant crops

In accordance with the laws of seasonal arrangements.

People should divide days, months and years,

As well as four seasons,

In order to grow crops well and strong.

Who could divide days, months and years?

Lord Gezi could divide them.

He divided a year into ten months,

He divided a month into forty days①.

---

① It is said in ancient time, human beings divided years, months and days in this wrong way.

分了年月日，
耪田种地收五谷，
年月分错了，
五谷不成熟。

怎样来算年？
怎样来算月？
怎样来算日？
房后有棵大松树，
一年长一台，
松树就是记年的。
房前有棵棕榈树，
一月发一匹，
棕树就是记月的。
地边有窝爬根草，
一天发一匹，
爬根草就是记日的。

年月日有了，
还没有四季。
怎样分四季？
河边杨柳发芽了，
大山梁子松树上，
布谷鸟儿声声叫，
大山大箐里，
李桂秧①叫起来了，

————————————

① 李桂秧：一种鸟的俗名。

144

After Lord Gezi divided days, months and years,

People began to plow fields and grow crops.

Lord Gezi divided years and months in a wrong way,

Crops thus were all immature.


How would people divide a year?

How would people divide a month?

How would people divide a day?

There was a big pine behind the house,

The pine grew one ring bigger each year,

People would use it for counting years.

There was a palm in front of the house,

The palm grew one more branch each month,

People would use it for counting months.

There was a clump of grass on the ground,

The clump of grass grew one more bunch each day,

People would use it for counting days.


Then years, months and days were separated,

But four seasons were not yet.

How would people separate four seasons?

When willows on riverbanks started to sprout,

When cuckoos started to sing

While sitting on those pines on high hills,

When Liguiyang① started to sing

While flying over mountains and valleys,

---

①　Liguiyang is a nickname of one kind of birds.

春季就到了。
河边水田里，
蛤蟆叫三声，
大山水箐里，
青蛙叫三声，
夏季就到了。
山上山下知了叫，
秋季就到了。
天心雁鹅飞
飞飞地上歇，
雁鹅叫三声，
冬季就到了。

算年月日的有了，
四季也分出来了，
从此大地上，
好耪庄稼了。

一年十二个月①，
月月要生产。
正月去背粪，
二月砍荞把，
三月撒荞子，
四月割大麦，

---

① 通过长期的生产实践，人类掌握了自然规律，于是正确的年、月、日就分出来了。

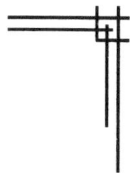

It was time for spring.

When toads began to croak

In the paddy fields by riversides,

When frogs began to croak

On mountains and valleys,

It was time for summer.

When cicadas started to sing over the mountains,

It was time for autumn.

When wild geese took a rest on the ground

While heading to the south,

When wild geese cried loud,

The winter came.


Then people had ways to divide years, months and days,

As well as four seasons.

Then people found it easier

To grow crops on earth.


There were twelve months in a year[1],

People had things to do every month.

They loaded manure in January,

They cut wheat straws in February,

They sowed buckwheat seeds in March,

They harvested barley in April,

---

[1] After years of agricultural production, human beings have mastered the law of nature and found out the correct ways to divide years, months and days.

五月忙栽秧，

六月去薅秧，

七月割苦荞，

八月割了谷子掰包谷，

九月割了甜荞撒大麦，

十月粮食装进仓，

冬月撒小麦，

腊月砍柴忙过年。

## 四、造工具

天神来吩咐，

耪田种庄稼。

庄稼哪个种？

庄稼哪个耪？

天王生的九个儿子，

地王生的七个姑娘。


没有造农具用的铁，

没有造农具用的铜，

到处去找铁，

到处去找铜。


哪个见铜花？

哪个见铁花？

山上的花鸟见铜花，

地上的岩蜂见铁花。

148

They planted rice in May,

They weeded paddy fields in June,

They harvested bitter buckwheat in July,

They harvested millet and corn in August,

They harvested sweet buckwheat and plant barley in September,

They stored grain into granary in October,

They sowed wheat seeds in November,

They chopped wood and get ready for the New Year in December.

# Section Four   Tool Making

Lord Gezi sent his orders,

About growing crops.

Who would plow fields?

Who would plant crops?

Lord Gezi's nine sons would do it,

Lord Gezi's seven daughters would do it.


But there was no iron to make farm tools,

And there was no copper to make farm tools.

People looked for iron everywhere,

People looked for copper everywhere.


Who had seen copper flowers before?

Who had seen iron flowers before?

A bird on a hill had seen copper flowers before,

A bee on the ground had seen iron flowers before.

早晨岩蜂去采花，
花鸟飞到石岩上。
岩蜂见到铁花了，
花鸟见到铜花了。

石岩下面铜水流，
石岩对面铁水淌，
拿也拿不起，
挨也挨不得。

哪个采铜花？
哪个采铁花？
阿查阿告颇①，
拿起竹帚扫铜花，
拿起竹帚扫铁花。
铜花烫得很，
铁花烫得很，
挨也挨不得，
扫也扫不起。

古时杀老虎，
剩下虎骨四小节，
拿来当扫帚，
扫下铜花来，
扫下铁花来。

———————————

①　阿查阿告颇：人名。

When the bee was gathering honey in morning,
It saw iron flowers.
When the bird was flying around rocks,
It saw copper flowers.

A copper stream went under rocks,
An iron stream went beside rocks.
But copper could not be touched,
And iron could not be taken.

Who would gather copper flowers?
Who would gather iron flowers?
Gaopo① would do it,
He took a bamboo broom to collect copper flowers,
He took a bamboo broom to collect iron flowers.
But copper flowers were too hot,
And could not be touched.
But iron flowers were too hot,
And could not be collected.

The tiger killed a long time ago
Left four small pieces of bones.
Gaopo took those bones as brooms
To collect copper flowers
And iron flowers.

---

① Gaopo: name of a man.

哪个先拣铜？
哪个先拣铁？
啄木鸟先拣铜，
啄木鸟先拣铁。
烫又烫得很，
甩又甩不掉。

人来拣铜，
人来拣铁。
剪下羊毛皮，
套在手指上，
脚上穿草鞋，
来拣铜和铁。

没有装铜的篮子，
没有装铁的篮子，
哪个找竹种？
哪个撒竹种？
门世地培阿①地方，
住着阿省莫若②，
阿省莫若有竹种，
阿底莫若③去要竹种。
阿底莫若找回竹种来，
撒到河边沙滩上。

---

① 门世地培阿：地名。
② 阿省莫若：人名。
③ 阿底莫若：人名。

Who would gather cooper?

Who would gather iron?

Woodpecker had a try first,

It tried to gather copper and iron.

Iron and copper were too hot,

Woodpecker failed to gather them.


Gaopo wanted to have a try,

He came to gather copper and iron.

He cut off a piece of sheep pelt first,

And wore it on his fingers as a glove.

He wore straw sandals on his feet,

And ready to gather iron and cooper.


There were no bamboo baskets to store the cooper he gathered,

There were no bamboo baskets to store the iron he gathered.

Who would look for bamboo seeds?

Who would sow bamboo seeds?

In a place called Menshidipei'a①,

There was a man called Ashengmoruo②,

Ashengmoruo had bamboo seeds.

Adimoruo③ went to ask for some.

Adimoruo brought some seeds back,

He sowed them on riverbanks.

---

① Menshidipei'a: name of a region.

② Ashengmoruo: name of a man.

③ Adimoruo: name of a man.

二月二十日，
竹种撒下了，
地头转一回，
地尾转一回，
已满十三日。
二轮二十五，
三轮三十七，
竹芽长得像鼠耳。

二月二十撒竹种，
三月二十日，
已满一个月，
四月二十日，
已满两个月，
竹子长成节。

栽竹子的季节到了，
栽竹子的日子到了，
哪个栽竹子？
阿底莫若栽竹子。
正是五月端阳节，
又是属猪栽竹日。
五月初五栽竹子，
六月初五满一月，

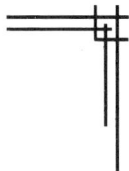

On February twentieth,

Bamboo seeds were sowed

On field head,

On field end.

Thirteen days passed,

Twenty-five days passed,

Thirty-seven days passed,

Bamboo sprouted and were like rat's ears.


Bamboo seeds were sowed on February twenty-second.

On March twentieth,

One month had passed.

On April twentieth,

Two months had passed.

Bamboo grew into small shoots.


It was the season to plant bamboo,

It was the day to plant bamboo.

Who would plant bamboo?

Adimoruo would do it.

It was the day of Dragon Boat Festival①,

And bamboo should be planted on the day of the pig.

Adimoruo planted bamboo on the fifth day of May,

One month had passed by June fifth,

---

① The Dragon Boat Festival is a traditional holiday originating in China, occurring near the summer solstice. The festival now occurs on the 5th day of the 5th month of the traditional Chinese calendar.

七月初五满两月，
栽下的竹子发了芽，
竹子长得绿莹莹。

哪个来壅土？
凤凰来壅土。
竹根壅上土，
竹子长得旺。

长到八月二十日，
长到九月二十日，
长到十月二十日，
长到冬月二十日，
长到腊月二十日，
长到正月二十日，
长到二月二十日，
栽下的竹子长成林，
栽下的竹子长得绿莹莹。

哪个来破竹？
胡高①来破竹。
破竹编篮子，
编成圆篮子，
拿来给马驮。

胡高又破竹，

---

① 胡高：人名。

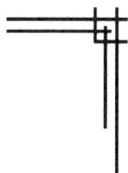

Two months had passed by July fifth,

The planted bamboo produced buds,

The planted bamboo grew very well.


Who would heap and fertilize earth around the bamboo roots?

The phoenix would do it.

When earth was heaped and fertilized,

Bamboo would grow well.


When it came to August twentieth,

When it came to September twentieth,

When it came to October twentieth,

When it came to November twentieth,

When it came to December twentieth,

When it came to January twentieth,

When it came to February twentieth,

The planted bamboo grew into bamboo forests,

The planted bamboo grew very well.


Who would cut bamboo?

Hugao① would cut bamboo.

He cut bamboo to weave baskets,

He wove round baskets,

These baskets could be put on horses' backs.


Hugao cut bamboo,

----

① Hugao: name of a man.

破竹声音沙沙响，
编成长篮子，
拿来给人背。

哪个来称铜？
告颇来称铜。
哪个来称铁？
告颇来称铁。
称好的铜铁装在篮子里。

铜铁称好了，
没有马来驮。
哪个来养马？
阿巴①来养马。
青草地上去放马，
草地放马马不壮；
河边去放马，
马吃河边象鼻草，
马就长膘壮起来。

正月二十日，
放马放到石坎上，
石坎下面有野牛，
马往石坎下面跑，

---

① 阿巴：人名。

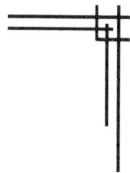

Making shasha sounds while cutting.

He wove long-shaped baskets,

These baskets could be put on people' backs.


Who would weigh copper?

Gaopo would weigh copper.

Who would weigh iron?

Gaopo would weigh iron.

He put weighed copper and iron into baskets.


Then copper and iron were well-weighed,

But people had no horse to carry them.

Who would raise horses?

Aba① would raise horses.

He herded horses on grasslands,

But horses did not eat well there.

He herded horses by the river,

Horses ate elephant trunk grass② there,

And grew well and strong.


On January twentieth,

When Aba herded a horse on a stone ridge,

There was a wild bull there.

When the horse ran into the wild bull,

---

① Aba: name of a man.
② Elephant trunk grass: name of a kind of grass.

牛往石坎上面跑。
野牛哞哞叫，
老马嘶嘶叫，
野牛配老马，
老马起驹了，
下了一匹小马驹，
准备来驮铜，
准备来驮铁。
驮铜驮铁驮不成，
成了皇帝状元骑的马。

布谷鸟儿叫，
又过一年了。
正月二十日，
母马起驹了，
生下一匹小骡子，
四脚镰刀花。
这回有骡子驮铜了，
这回有骡子驮铁了。

鸡树板做鞍头，
青菜皮树做鞍板，
橡子做架子，

When the wild bull ran into the horse,

The wild bull barked "moumou",

The old horse barked "sisi".

They mated.

The old horse got pregnant,

And gave birth to a little horse.

The little horse could carry copper,

The little horse could carry iron,

But it did not, instead,

It became a horse carrying emperors and Zhuangyuan①.


When cuckoos sang again,

One year had passed.

On January twentieth,

A female horse got pregnant,

And gave birth to a mule

Whose feet could withstand knife's cut.

Now people had mules to carry cooper,

Now people had mules to carry iron.


People used Jishu② wood to make a saddle head,

People used Qingcaipi wood to make a saddle body,

People used oak wood to make a saddle frame,

---

① Zhuangyuan is the champion in Chinese imperial examinations. Chinese imperial examinations were a civil service examination system in imperial China to select candidates for the state bureaucracy.

② Jishu: name of a tree.

树皮做架绳，

枫树做楸珠，

枫树做楸网，

棕皮做硬褡，

獐子皮做软褡，

配好鞍架驮铜铁。

哪个来赶马？

俄考①来赶马。

俄考力气大，

端起驮子不费劲。


驮着铜铁下坡坡，

石头挡在路当中，

哪个来开路？

七月下大雨，

到处淌山水，

山水滚滚流，

路当中的石头都冲走。


驮着铜铁过横路，

大树挡在路当中，

哪个来开路？

啄木鸟来开路。

---

① 俄考：人名。

People used oak bark to make rope,

People used maple wood to make joints,

People used maple wood to make nets,

People used palm bark to make a hard saddle pad,

People used river deer's skins to make a soft saddle pad,

Now the mule was well equipped with the saddle.

Who would lead the mule?

Ekao① would lead the mule.

He had great strength,

He could take up the load easily.


The mule went along a downward slope,

Carrying the load of cooper and iron.

They found a stone blocking the way.

Who would clear it away?

Heavy rain of July poured everywhere,

It washed all mountains and roads,

It washed the stone away.


The mule went along a road, carrying the load of cooper and

iron,

They found a tree blocking the way.

Who would clear it away?

The woodpecker would clear it away.

---

① Ekao: name of a man.

驮着铜铁坡上走，
石坎挡在坡当中，
哪个来开路？
穿山甲来开路。

道路开通了，
驮着铜铁到处走，
四面八方走遍了，
没有打铜的人，
没有打铁的人。

驮到四川峨眉山，
驮到云南滇池边，
没有会打刀的人，
没有会打农具的人。

驮到永仁去，
走过仁和街，
只听叮当打铁声，
不见铁匠是哪个。

The mule went along an upward slope,
They found a stone ridge blocking the way.
Who would clear it away?
The pangolin would clear it away.

The ways were all cleared,
They were able to get around and go anywhere
With the load of cooper and iron.
Yet there was no blacksmith,
And there was no coppersmith.

They went to Mount Emei① in Sichuan,
They went to Lake Dianchi② in Yunnan.
Yet there was nobody who could make knives,
And there was nobody who could make agricultural tools.

They went to Yongren County③,
They went through Renhe Street.
They only heard sounds of "dingdang" of iron-forging,
But did not find a blacksmith.

---

① Mount Emei is a mountain in Sichuan Province, China, and is one of the Four Sacred Buddhist Mountains of China.
② Lake Dianchi is a large lake located on the Yunnan-Guizhou Plateau close to Kunming, Yunnan Province, China.
③ Yongren County is a county in Chuxiong Autonomous District in Yunnan Provicnce, with the highest population of Yi people.

驮到中和、直苴①去，
没有会打锄头的人，
没有会打镰刀的人。

驮到大村②去，
驮到茨拉去，
没有打铜打铁的人。

驮到白草岭③，
驮到宾川城，
没有打铜打铁的人。

驮到盐丰去，
驮到姚安去，
没有打铜打铁的人。
驮回六苴④来，
还是找不到。
驮到大理苍山顶，
驮到永昌城。

---

① 中和、直苴：村名，在大姚县。
② 大村：村名，在大姚县。
③ 白草岭：山名，是楚雄彝族自治州最高的山，海拔三千六百米。
④ 六苴：地名，在大姚县。

They went to Zhonghe and Zhiju Village①,
But they found nobody who could make hoes
And nobody who could make reaping hocks.

They went to Dacun Village②,
They went to Cila Village③,
But they found nobody who could forge iron or copper.

They went to Mount Baicao④,
They went to Binchuan County⑤,
But they found nobody who could forge iron or copper.

They went to Yanfeng County⑥,
They went to Yao'an County⑦,
But they found nobody who could forge iron or copper.

They went back to Liuju⑧,
But they found nobody who could forge iron or copper.
They went to Mount Cangshan in Dali Region,
They went to Yongchang⑨.

---

① Zhonghe, Zhiju are names of villages in Dayao County. Dayao is also a county in Chuxiong Autonomous District in Yunnan Provicnce, with a large population of Yi people.

② Dacun: name of a village in Dayao County.

③ Cila: name of a village in Dayao County.

④ Mount Baicao is the highest mountain in Chuxiong Autonomous District in Yunnan Provicnce, with a height of about 3,600 meters.

⑤ Binchuan County is a county in Dali District in Yunnan Province.

⑥ Yanfeng and Yaoan are county names.

⑦ Yanfeng and Yaoan are county names.

⑧ Liuju: name of a village in Dayao County.

⑨ Yongchang: name of a region in Yunnan Province.

蒙化出铁，
东川出铜，
沙拉出好铅，
就是没有打铜打铁的人。

驮着铜铁到牟定，
路上听见马鹿叫，
走过牟定岔路口，
看见打死很多鹿。
牟定城外有条河，
有姑娘在河边洗衣服。
马鹿被打得叫，
跳进水里到处游。

进了牟定城，
有了打铜的人，
有了打铁的人，
有了铸锅的人。
马鹿头拿来做砧，
马鹿角拿来做锥，
马鹿脚拿来做钳子，
马鹿身子做风箱，
开始打铜打铁了。

Menghua① had an iron mine,

Dongchuan② had a copper mine,

Shala③ had a lead mine,

But there was nobody there who could forge iron or copper.


They went to Mouding④,

And heard bowing sounds made by red deer.

They went across a road,

And saw many dead red deer.

They passed by a river outside the city,

And saw a girl washing clothes by the river.

They also saw a red deer being beaten hard and making "miemie" sounds,

They saw it jumping into the river and trying to run away.


After they entered Mouding City,

They found people who could forge copper,

They found people who could forge iron,

They found people who could make pots.

They found heads of red deer being taken to make hammering blocks,

They found horns of red deer being taken to make awls,

They found feet of red deer being taken to make pliers,

They found bodies of red deer being taken to make bellows,

They finally found someone who could forge iron or copper.

---

① Menghua: name of a region in Yunnan Province.

② Dongchuan: name of a region in Yunnan Province.

③ Shala: name of a region in Yunnan Province.

④ Mouding: name of a region in Yunnan Province.

铜的用处多得很，
铁的用处多得很，
打出铁来一团团，
铁团丢进冷水里，
再从水里拿出来，
拿出就能做工具。

先打犁头三大把，
用来开田种庄稼；
后打镰刀三大把，
用来割谷子；
再打一把锯，
拿来锯木板；
打了锯子打剪刀，
剪布裁衣有工具。
工具都打好了，
九个儿子拿着农具种庄稼，
七个姑娘背着刀子放牛羊。

正月过新年，
二月三月过去了，
五月端午来，
九个儿子看见橡子林，
看见赤松青松林。

Copper was used widely,

Iron was used widely.

Finished iron was like balls,

If people threw iron balls into cold water,

And then took them out,

Iron balls could be made into tools.

People made three plowshares first,

And took them to plow fields.

People made three reaping hooks,

And took them to reap crops.

People made a saw,

And took it to cut wooden boards.

People made scissors,

And took them to cut out clothes.

Having all the tools created,

The nine sons took them to plant crops,

The seven daughters took them to herd cattle.

The New Year was in January,

Then February and March followed,

When Dragon Boat Festival came in May,

The Nine sons saw oak woods,

Green pine woods and red pine woods.

到了五月天，
一天三次雨，
橡子树砍来做犁架，
安上铁犁头，
水牛黄牛架起来，
脖子架弯担，
拴上皮索子。

六月二十属龙日，
开始犁生地：
水冬瓜树下犁荞地，
砍下水冬瓜树枝烧荞地；
松树底下撒甜荞，
松树砍来烧荞地。
荞子长得好，
颗颗像葡萄。

## 五、盐

男人服侍树，
女人服侍草；
树叶不残缺，
青草长得旺；
野兽不会来，
雀鸟不离窝；
高山好放羊，
白羊遍山冈。

In May,

It rained three times a day.

People cut oak trees to make plow frames,

And equipped frames with iron plowshares.

People ordered buffaloes and bulls to take plow frames,

And equipped buffaloes and bulls with curved poles

And leather ropes.


People began to plow virgin fields

On June twentieth, a day of the dragon.

People plowed buckwheat fields under Shuidonggua trees,

They burned Shuidonggua branches to fertilize the fields.

People sowed sweet buckwheat seeds under pine trees,

They burned pine branches to fertilize the fields.

Buckwheat grew well and strong,

Grain looked like grapes.

## Section Five　Salt

Men were responsible for cultivating trees,

Women were responsible for cultivating grass.

All tree leaves were protected well,

All grass grew well.

Beasts did not disturb people,

Birds did not leave their own nests.

Mountains were good for sheep herding,

White sheep were herded all over the mountains.

山坡去放羊，
一只大绵羊不见了！
山山箐箐都找遍，
找来找去找不到。

三十三天后，
绵羊回来了。
绵羊回羊群，
羊群围拢来；
羊群围着大绵羊，
去它身上舔。

放羊老人起疑心，
手摸羊毛嘴里尝，
心里自思量：
"大绵羊身上有咸味，
大绵羊一定吃了盐巴水，
看看盐水在哪方。"
老人拿来铁链子，
小心拴在羊脚上，
看看绵羊去哪方。

大绵羊沿着山下走，
一走走到安丰井；

People went to herd sheep on a slope,

But they found one sheep disappeared.

They searched over all mountains and valleys,

But failed to find the missing sheep.


Thirty-three days passed,

The lost sheep came home.

When it went back to the flock,

Other sheep gathered around.

They gathered around the big sheep,

Licking its wool.


The old shepherd was curious about it.

He touched its wool and tasting it,

He had an epiphany:

"Its wool tastes salty.

The sheep must have drunk salty water somewhere.

I will find out where salty water is."

Then the old shepherd took out an iron chain,

And tied it to the foot of the sheep,

Intending to find out where the sheep would go.


The big sheep walked down along the mountain,

And got to Well Anfeng①.

---

①　Anfeng: name of a well.

继续往上走，
走到白盐井。
一片大森林，
林密草又深，
林中淌盐水，
兽类围水边，
舔水吃盐巴。
老人跟着绵羊走，
看见盐水笑眯眯。

河头写字贴上，
河尾插上木牌；
各族人一起跑来看，
都说真是好盐水。

傈僳族来煮盐，
没有煮成功。
汉族来煮盐，
头回煮不成，
后来仔细想，
二回煮成了。

大家听说煮出盐，
纷纷搬到石羊来。

The sheep kept going forward,

And got to Well Baiyan①.

There was a big forest

With dense woods and deep grass,

There was salty water flowing through the forest,

There were beasts gathering

And drinking along the water.

The old shepherd followed this sheep,

And were delighted when finding the salty water.


The old shepherd put up a notice at the river's head,

As well as a wooden board at the river's end.

People of all ethnic groups got the message and came to see,

They all said it was good salty water.


Lisu people came to produce salt,

But they did not succeed.

Han people came to produce salt,

But they did not succeed for the first time.

After thinking over and over,

They tried again and successfully produced salt this time.


After hearing salt was successfully produced,

People all moved to Shiyang②.

---

① Baiyan: name of a well.

② Shiyang: name of a region which is famous for salt production.

山坡有荞子，
山上有大麻，
平坝有谷子，
平坝有小麦，
人户增多了，
变成石羊镇①。
牧羊老人看见了，
望着四山眯眯笑。

## 六、蚕丝

东洋大海石岩边，
柞桑树有三林，
甜桑树有三林，
马桑树有三林。
天神撒下蚕种来，
一撒撒在树桠上。
桑树底下三堆屎，
江西挑担人，
来到桑树下，
看见了蚕屎，
找到了蚕种。

蚕种找着了，
哪个抱②蚕子？
汉家姑娘抱蚕子。

---

① 石羊镇：地名，又叫白井，出盐的地方。
② 抱：孵化的意思。

梅葛 Meige

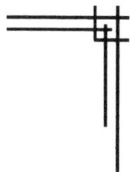

They grew buckwheat on slopes,

They grew flax on mountains,

They grew crops in flatlands,

They grew wheat in flatlands,

With an increasing population,

Shiyang became a big town.

The old shepherd was delighted,

He was pleased to see people's good life.

## Section Six　Silk

Around those rocks by the Eastern Sea,

There were three wild mulberry trees,

There were three sweet mulberry trees,

There were three coriaria mulberry trees.

Lord Gezi sprinkled silkworm eggs

On the branches of those mulberry trees.

Silkworm excrement piled under mulberry trees.

A carrier from Jiangxi① passed by,

He noticed the silkworm excrement

Under those trees,

And found silkworm eggs.

Silkworm eggs were found,

But who would hatch them?

Han② young women would hatch them.

①　Jiangxi: name of a province in China.

②　Han is China's main nationality. Han people are distributed all over the country.

三年闰一月，
一年打两春。
打春后三天，
桑树发出来，
蚕儿钻出来。

蚕有了，
桑叶也有了，
没有簸箕和筛子，
怎么来养蚕。
去找竹子来，
去请篾匠来，
把簸箕编出来，
把筛子编出来。
蚕养在簸箕筛子里。

要扫蚕了，
一天扫三回，
三天扫九回。
怎样喂蚕？
先喂什么？

Leap year reoccured every four years,

There were two springs in this year.

On the third day after the Beginning of Spring①,

Mulberry trees started to grow,

And silkworms started to hatch from eggs.


There were silkworms,

And there were mulberry leaves,

But there were no Boji or Saizi,

How would people raise silkworms?

People went to get bamboo,

People went to find bamboo craftsman.

Craftsman would make Boji,

Craftsman would make Saizi,

Then silkworms were raised in Boji and Saizi.


People cleaned Boji and Saizi for silkworms,

People cleaned them three times a day,

People cleaned them nine times in three days.

How would people feed silkworms?

What should be fed first?

---

①　The Beginning of Spring, the first solar term of the year. The traditional Chinese lunar calendar divides the year into 24 solar terms. The 24 solar terms, based on the sun's position in the zodiac, were created by farmers in ancient China to guide the agricultural affairs and farming activities. The 24 solar terms reflect the changes in climate, natural phenomena, agricultural production, and other aspects of human life, including clothing, food, housing, and transportation.

后喂什么？
先喂柞桑叶，
再喂甜桑叶，
后喂马桑叶，
蚕就养大了。

哪个来拣蚕？
汉家姑娘来拣蚕。
一天拣三回，
三天拣九回。
小的拣一堆，
大的拣一堆。
小的拣在簸箕里，
大的拣在筛垫上。
小的一天喂一次，
大的一天喂三次。

蚕养老了，
没有吐丝的地方。
汉家田埂上，
长着茴香草。
割来茴香草，
把蚕放草上。
属羊日吐丝，
蚕茧结成了。

What should be fed next?
Wild mulberry leaves would be fed first,
Sweet mulberry leaves would be fed next,
Coriaria mulberry leaves would be fed last,
Silkworms grew.

Who would select silkworms?
Han young women would select silkworms.
They did it three times a day,
They did it nine times in three days.
Small silkworms were gathered into one group,
Big ones were collected into another group.
Small silkworms were put in Boji,
Big ones were put in Saizi.
Small silkworms were fed once a day,
Big ones were fed three times a day.

Silkworms grew old,
But there was nowhere for them to spin silk.
There was fennel grass
On the field ridges owned by Han people.
People cut fennel grass,
And put silkworms on it.
Silkworms spun silk on a day of the sheep,
And people finally got silkworm cocoons.

大理铁锣锅，
昆明大铁锅，
用来煮蚕茧。
哪个来挑丝线？
哪个来纺丝线？
剑川人用黄竹筷子挑蚕丝，
剑川人纺丝线。

蚕丝挑出来，
丝线纺出来，
白茧纺出白丝线，
红茧纺出红丝线，
黄茧纺出黄丝线，
各色丝线都纺好，
用它来绣花衣裳。

There were iron pots in Dali,

There were iron pots in Kunming[1],

The iron pots were used to boil silkworm cocoons.

Who would harvest silk thread?

Who would spin silk thread?

Jianchuan people would harvest silk thread with bamboo chopsticks,

Jianchuan people would spin silk thread.


People harvested silk thread,

They spun silk thread

People made white silk out of white silkworm cocoons,

They made red silk out of red silkworm cocoons,

They made yellow silk out of yellow silkworm cocoons.

People made silk of all colors,

They made beautiful clothes.

---

[1] Kunming, name of a region in Yunnan Province, now is the provinical capital of Yunnan.

# 第三部　婚事和恋歌

## 一、相配

八月十五，
天王降下历书来，
汉族写字在书上，
四面八方都传到，
传遍各地方。

到了正月二十日，
汉家姑娘去背土，
男人拿土做春牛，
做出春牛是黄嘴，
做出春牛脚也黄，
做出春牛手也黄。

正月二十五，
春牛做成了，
人人迎春牛，
抬着春牛闹哄哄，

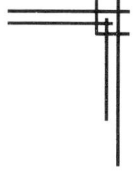

# Chapter Three   Love Affairs and Marriages

## Section One   Match

On August the fifteenth,

Lord Gezi gave people an almanac,

He asked Han people to write on it.

People passed it around,

People passed it around the world.


On January twentieth,

Han young women went to carry clay,

And men would make a clay bull.

Men made yellow clay mouth,

Men made yellow clay feet,

Men made yellow clay limbs.


On January twenty-fifth,

A clay bull was successfully made.

People all went out to welcome it,

They carried it happily along the streets.

芦笙吹一对，
唢呐吹一对，
笛子吹一对，
跳神匠来一对，
街头到街尾，
吹吹唱唱迎春牛，
春牛赶下河，
从此春风吹起来。

春风吹到河两岸，
河边柳树先发芽。
吹到白樱桃树上，
白樱桃树就发芽。
吹到松林里，
松树就发芽。
吹到桃李梨树上，
桃李梨树就发芽。
吹到高山柏树上，
柏树就发芽。
吹到罗汉松树上，
罗汉松树就发芽。

People played Lusheng①,

They played Suona②,

They played flute,

They invited dance players to perform.

People welcomed the clay bull,

While playing and singing all the way along the streets.

Afterwards people pushed the clay bull into river,

And spring wind began to blow everafter.


When spring wind blew to the riverbanks,

Willow trees sprouted afterwards.

When spring wind blew to the white cherry trees,

Cherry trees began to sprout.

When spring wind blew to the pine woods,

Pines started to grow new shoots.

When spring wind blew to the peaches and plums,

Peaches and plums began to sprout.

When spring wind blew to the cypress trees on those high

mountains,

Cypress trees started to grow new shoots.

When spring wind blew to the Buddhist pines,

Buddhist pines began to sprout.

---

① Lusheng is a Chinese traditional musical instrument with multiple bamboo pipes, each fitted with a free reed, which are fitted into a long blowing tube made of hardwood.

② Suona is a Chinese traditional musical instrument. It has a distinctively loud and high-pitched sound, and is used frequently in Chinese traditional music ensembles, particularly those that perform outdoors.

吹到草<u>丛</u>里，
百草就发芽。
没有不发芽的树，
没有不发芽的草。
世间万物都发芽，
发芽要开花。
八月十五到，
日月就开花。
十冬腊月到，
星星就开花。
六月七月到，
白云黑云朵朵开。
正二三月到，
风吹百花开。
天花开来落地上，
大山小山鲜花开，
河边坝子鲜花开，
四面八方鲜花开。

什么是树王？
白樱桃树是树王。
白樱桃树开了花，
花瓣吹落刺树上，
大小刺树鲜花开。
花蕊落在青松赤松上，
青松赤松开了花。
落在柏枝梢梢上，
柏枝梢梢也开花。

When spring wind blew to the grass,

Grass started to grow new shoots.

All trees produced new leaves,

All grass produced new buds,

All plants sprouted well,

All plants were ready to bloom.

On August the fifteenth,

The sun and the moon came into bloom.

In November and December in winter,

Stars came into bloom.

In June and July in summer,

White and black clouds came into bloom.

In Feberary and March in spring,

All flowers were in full bloom.

Heaven flowers dropped on the ground,

Mountain flowers were all around,

All flowers by riversides and in flatlands were in full bloom,

Flowers everywhere were all in full bloom.


What tree was the king of trees?

White cherry was the king of trees.

After its blossom,

Its petals were blown to the thorn tree,

The thorn tree then came into bloom.

Its stamens dropped on green pine and red pine,

And the green pine and red pine came into bloom.

Its flowers dropped on top of the cypress tree,

And the cypress tree came into bloom.

落在香橄木树根根上，
香橄木树也开花。
落在芭蕉上，
芭蕉也开花。
落在箐中水沟里，
水沟边上树开花。
落在马缨花树上，
马缨花树也开花。
落到坝区山腰里，
花红梨树也开花。
吹到梧桐树上，
梧桐树也开花。
吹到河边两岸上，
柳树也开花。
树木开完花，
草也想开花。

什么是草王？
芦苇是草王。
芦苇先开花，
花瓣吹到山中毒草根根上，
毒草就开花。
吹到山竹根根上，
大小山竹都开花。
吹到河边艾草根根上，
艾草也开花。
吹到黄麻上，

Its flowers dropped on roots of the olive tree,

And the olive tree came into bloom.

Its flowers dropped on the banana tree,

And the banana tree came into bloom.

Its flowers dropped into the valleys,

And all trees along the valleys came into bloom.

Its flowers dropped on the Mayinghua tree,

And the Mayinghua tree came into bloom.

Its flowers dropped on hill sides in the flatlands,

And the red flower and pear tree came into bloom.

Spring wind blew its flowers to the phoenix tree,

And the phoenix tree came into bloom.

Spring wind blew its flowers to the riverbanks,

And the willow tree came into bloom.

When all trees began to bloom,

Grass wanted to bloom as well.


What grass was the king of grass?

Reed was the king of grass.

Reed came into bloom first,

Spring wind blew its flowers to poisonous weeds in the
mountains,

And the poisonous weeds came into bloom.

Spring wind blew its flowers to mangosteen roots,

And the mangosteens came into bloom.

Spring wind blew its flowers to wormwood roots by riversides,

And the wormwood came into bloom.

Spring wind blew its flowers to Huangma,

黄麻也开花。
没有不开花的树，
没有不开花的草。

一轮一十三，
二轮二十六，
一个月开花，
一个月不开花。
树开完了花，
草开完了花；
树木开的花落了，
草儿开的花落了。

什么是兽王？
兔子是兽王。
兔子先开花，
吹到老虎老熊脊背上，
老虎老熊也开花。
吹到狐狸黄鼠狼头上，
狐狸黄鼠狼也开花。
吹到马鹿岩羊头顶上，
马鹿岩羊也开花。
吹到獐子麂子头顶上，
獐子麂子也开花。
吹到松鼠头顶上，
松鼠也开花。
吹到河头鱼窝里，

And the Huangma began to blossom.

There were no trees that did not bloom,

There was no grass that did not bloom.


One round of thirteen days had passed,

Two rounds of twenty-six days had passed,

All plants were in blossom in one month,

All plants were not in blossom in the next month.

All trees bloomed,

All grass bloomed.

All trees fell,

All grass fell.


What animal was the king of animals?

Rabbit was the king of animals.

The rabbit began to blossom first,

Spring wind blew its flowers to tiger and bear's backs,

And the tiger and bear began to blossom.

Spring wind blew its flowers to fox and yellow weasel's heads,

And the fox and yellow weasel began to blossom.

Spring wind blew its flowers to red deer and blue sheep's

heads,

And the red deer and blue sheep began to blossom.

Spring wind blew its flowers to river deer and muntjac's heads,

And the river deer and muntjac began to blossom.

Spring wind blew its flowers to squirrel's head,

And the squirrel began to blossom.

Spring wind blew its flowers to fish's head,

鱼也开了花。
吹到石蚌头顶上，
石蚌也开花。
没有不开花的兽，
没有不开花的鸟。

什么是鸟王？
凤凰是鸟王。
凤凰先开花，
吹到大雁头顶上，
大雁就开花。
吹到岩鸡头顶上，
岩鸡也开花。
吹到老鸹喜鹊头顶上，
老鸹喜鹊也开花。
吹到斑鸠头顶上，
斑鸠也开花。

吹到啄木鸟头上，
啄木鸟也开花。
吹到布谷鸟头上，
布谷鸟也开花。
吹到李桂秧头上，
李桂秧也开花。
没有不开花的鸟。

家禽耕畜要开花。
春风吹到骒马头顶上，

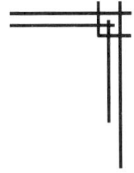

And the fish began to blossom.

Spring wind blew its flowers to stone clam's head,

And the stone clam began to blossom.

There were no beasts that did not bloom,

There were no birds that did not bloom.


What bird was the king of birds?

Phoenix was the king of birds.

The phoenix began to blossom first,

Spring wind blew its flowers to wild goose's head,

And the wild goose began to blossom.

Spring wind blew its flowers to wild rooster's head,

And the wild rooster began to blossom.

Spring wind blew its flowers to crow and magpie's heads,

And the crow and magpie began to blossom.

Spring wind blew its flowers to turtledove's head,

And the turtledove began to blossom.


Spring wind blew its flowers to woodpecker's head,

And the woodpecker began to blossom.

Spring wind blew its flowers to cuckoo's head,

And the cuckoo began to blossom.

Spring wind blew its flowers to Liguiyang,

And the Liguiyang began to blossom.

There was no bird that did not blossom.


Poultry and livestock would blossom.

Spring wind blew its flowers to mule and horse's heads,

骡子和马都开花。
吹到水牛头顶上，
水牛也开花。
吹到绵羊山羊头顶上，
绵羊山羊也开花。
吹到公鸡母鸡头顶上，
公鸡母鸡也开花。
吹到鹅鸭头顶上，
鹅鸭也开花。
吹到门外狗头上，
狗也开了花。
吹到屋里猫头上，
猫也开了花。
没有不开花的耕畜，
没有不开花的家禽。

树开花了，
草也开花了，
百兽开花了，
百鸟也开花了，
家禽开花了，
耕畜也开花了，
没有不开花的草木，
没有不开花的鸟兽。
草木鸟兽开完花，
人类忙着把花开。

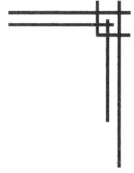

And the mule and horse began to blossom.

Spring wind blew its flowers to buffalo's head,

And the buffalo began to blossom.

Spring wind blew its flowers to sheep and goat's heads,

And the sheep and goat began to blossom.

Spring wind blew its flowers to rooster and hen's heads,

And the rooster and hen began to blossom.

Spring wind blew its flowers to goose and duck's head,

And the goose and duck began to blossom.

Spring wind blew its flowers to dog's head which was out of
the door,

And the dog began to blossom.

Spring wind blew its flowers to cat's head which was inside
the house,

And the cat began to blossom.

There was no livestock which did not bloom,

There was no poultry which did not bloom.


Trees began to bloom,

Grass began to bloom,

Beasts began to bloom,

Birds began to bloom,

Poultry began to bloom,

Livestock began to bloom.

There were no trees or grass which did not blossom,

There were no birds or beasts which did not blossom.

After plants, birds and beasts bloomed,

Human beings began to blossom.

春风吹到傣族头顶上，
傣族也开花。
吹到高山彝族头顶上，
彝族也开花。
吹到坝子里的汉族头顶上，
汉族也开花。
吹到回族头顶上，
回族也开花。
吹到擀毡匠头上，
擀毡的人也开花。
吹到高山庙里和尚头顶上，
和尚也开花。

百草百木都开花，
百鸟百兽都开花，
世人都开花，
开花结果要相配。
八月十五到，
日月就相配。
吃了什么来相配？
吃了金玉珠宝来相配。
十冬腊月到，
大星小星配。
吃了什么东西来相配？
吃了寒霜露水来相配。

Spring wind blew its flowers to Dai people,

And the Dai people began to blossom.

Spring wind blew its flowers to Yi people living in the high

mountains,

And the Yi people began to blossom.

Spring wind blew its flowers to Han people living in the

flatlands,

And the Han people began to blossom.

Spring wind blew its flowers to Hui people,

And the Hui people began to blossom.

Spring wind blew its flowers to carpet craftsman,

And the carpet craftsman began to blossom.

Spring wind blew its flowers to monks living in temple in

high mountains,

And the monks began to blossom.


All grass and trees bloomed,

All birds and beasts bloomed,

People bloomed,

They needed mating to yield after blossom.

On August the fifteenth,

The sun mated with the moon.

What did they eat before mating?

They ate precious things like gold and pearls.

In November and December of winter days,

Big stars mated with small stars.

What did they eat before mating?

They ate frost and dew.

六月七月天，
白云黑云来相配。
正二三月到，
春风空气来相配。
天要地来配，
地要树来配。

天上吹来一阵风，
吹到河当中，
风和水波配。
河配岩来岩配石，
岩石又和树相配。
柿树梨树两相配，
罗汉松和大风配。

什么是兽王？
兔子是兽王。
兔子吃了什么来相配？
吃了小麦来相配。
什么兽力气最大？
老虎力气最大。
老虎吃了什么来相配？
吃了小兽来相配。
豺狼吃了什么来相配？
吃了羊子来相配。
黄鼠狼吃了什么来相配？
吃了蜂子来相配。

In June and July of summer days,
White clouds mated with black.
In February and March of new year's days,
Spring wind mated with spring air.
The sky mated with the earth,
The earth mated with trees.

Wind blew down from the sky above,
And it blew over rivers.
Wind mated with river waves.
Rivers mated with rocks,
Rocks mated with stones,
Rocks mated with trees too.
Persimmon trees mated with pear trees.
Buddhist pines mated with strong wind too.

What animal was the king of animals?
Rabbits were the king of animals.
What did they eat before mating?
Rabbits ate wheat before mating.
What beast had the greatest strength?
Tigers had the greatest strength.
What did tigers eat before mating?
Tigers ate small beasts before mating.
What did jackals eat before mating?
jackals ate sheep before mating.
What did yellow weasels eat before mating?
Yellow weasels ate bees before mating.

岩羊吃了什么来相配？
吃了岩草来相配。
野猪要相配，
拱地吃树根来相配。
大熊小熊来相配，
吃了苦葛根来相配。
没有不相配的兽，
就连地上的蚂蚁都相配。

什么是鸟王？
凤凰是鸟王。
凤凰要相配，
吃了什么来相配？
吃了小虫来相配。
大雁吃了什么便相配？
吃了坝子里的黄谷便相配。
老鹰吃了什么便相配？
吃了蚂蚁竹鸡便相配。
斑鸠吃了什么就相配？
吃了樱桃果子就相配。
麻雀要相配，
吃了谷子来相配。
没有不相配的鸟。

虫虫也相配，
先是蚂蚁配。
蚂蚁吃了什么来相配？
吃了粮食来相配。

What did blue sheep eat before mating?

Blue sheep ate rockweed before mating.

Boars would mate,

They ate tree roots before mating.

Big bears and small bears would mate,

They ate the bitter roots of the kudzu vine before mating.

There were no beasts which did not mate,

Even those ants on the ground would mate.


What bird was the king of birds?

Phoenix was the king of birds.

Phoenix would mate,

What would phoenix eat before mating?

They ate little worms before mating.

What would wild geese eat before mating?

They ate yellow millet before mating.

What would eagles eat before mating?

They ate ants and bamboo partridges before mating.

What would turtledoves eat before mating?

They ate cherries before mating.

Sparrows would mate,

They ate millet before mating.

There were no birds which did not mate.


Insects and worms would mate,

Ants would mate first.

What would ants eat before mating?

They ate grain before mating.

蚯蚓来相配，
吃了什么来相配？
吃了泥土来相配。

大蛇来相配，
吃了什么来相配？
吃了蚯蚓来相配。
蜜蜂吃了什么配？
吃了花蕊来相配。
没有不相配的树木花草，
没有不相配的鸟兽虫鱼，
没有不相配的人。
样样东西都相配，
地上的东西才不绝。

天有天的规：
白云嫁黑云；
月亮嫁太阳；
天嫁给地；
男女相配，
人间才成对。

## 二、说亲

男：我家里没有女，
我家里没有花；
我的心里急，
我的心里慌；

Earthworms would mate,

What would earthworms eat before mating?

They ate mud before mating.

What would snakes eat before mating?

They ate earthworms before mating.

What would bees eat before mating?

They ate stamen and pistil before mating.

There were no trees or flowers which did not mate,

There were no beasts or birds which did not mate,

There were no human beings who did not mate.

Everyone would mate,

So as to reproduce new generations.

The sky had its rules and norms.

White clouds would mate with black clouds,

The moon would mate with the sun,

The sky would mate with the earth,

Women would mate with men,

People would make couples then.

## Section Two　Matchmaking

MAN: There are no daughters in our family,

There are no flowers in our family.

I am concerned,

I am worried.

要向你家讨个女，
要向你家要朵花，
请你答应给我家。

女：你家没有女，
你家没有花；
要向我家讨，
要女又要花。
请你别处找，
请你别家讨；
我家没有女，
我家没有花。

男：你一定说没有女，
你一定说没有花，
这么说起来，
我的心里慌。
怎么没有女？
怎么没有花？
我家小花猫，
去你家偷肉吃，
小花猫看见了，
你家有个女，
你家有朵花。
我家小黑狗，
舔你家姑娘的围裙，
小黑狗也看见了，
你家有个女，
你家有朵花。

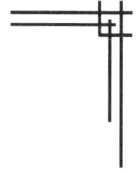

I want to ask you for your daughter,

I want to ask you for your flower.

Please offer us a promise.


WOMAN: There are no daughters in your family,

There are no flowers in your family.

You ask our family for one,

You ask our family for a daughter and a flower.

Please go ask others,

Please go ask other families.

There are no daughters in our family,

There are no flowers in our family.


MAN: No wonder you would say you had no daughter,

No wonder you would say you had no flower.

When hearing this,

I am so upset.

Do not you have a daughter?

Do not you have a flower?

When my kitten went to your house

To steal meat to eat,

It saw your daughter,

And it saw your flower.

It saw them.

When my black puppy licked the apron of your daughter,

It saw your daughter,

And it saw your flower.

It saw them.

你家小姑娘，
一定给我家。

女：你一定要向我家讨女，
你一定要向我家要花；
我家没有女，
我家没有花。
你家小花猫，
只会偷肉吃，
它不会说话，
它没有看见女，
它没有看见花。
你家小黑狗，
只会舔围裙，
它也不会说话，
它没有看见女，
它没有看见花。
我家没有女，
我家没有花，
请你别村去讨女，
请你别村去要花。

男：你说你家没有女，
你说你家没有花？
三个葫芦蜂，
来到你家采露水，
看见你家有朵花。
三窝小蜜蜂，

We ask you for your daughter,

Please offer us your daughter.


WOMAN: You insist to ask me for my daughter,

You insist to ask me for my flower,

But I have not any daughter,

Nor any flower.

The kitten of yours,

Only knows how to steal meat,

But does not know how to speak.

It did not see my daughter,

It did not see my flower.

The black puppy of yours,

Only knows how to lick,

But does not know how to speak.

It did not see my daughter,

It did not see my flower.

I do not have a daughter,

I do not have a flower,

Please go to other villages for daughters,

Please go to other villages for flowers.


MAN: You said you do not have a daughter,

You said you do not have a flower.

Three bumblebees

Saw your flower,

When gathering honey around your house.

Three swarms of bees,

飞到你家来采花，
看见你家有个小姑娘。
你家有女又有花，
请你答应给我家。

女：你说三窝小蜜蜂，
看见我家有个小姑娘？
你说三个葫芦蜂，
见着我家有朵花？
它是来采露水，
它是来采花，
它说的不是实话。
我家没有小姑娘，
我家没有花。
处处是村子，
请你别家去找花。

男：你家躲着女，
你家藏着花。
江西货郎哥，
卖针卖线到你家，
你家小姑娘，
爱针又爱线。
货郎看见了，
货郎跟我说，
货郎跟我讲，
你家有个小姑娘。
躲也躲不住，

Saw your daughter,

When collecting pollen around your house.

You have a daughter and you have a flower,

Please offer us a promise.


WOMAN: You said that

Three swarms of bees saw my daughter,

You said that

Three bumblebees saw my flower.

They came to gather honey only,

They came to collect pollen only,

They did not tell you the truth.

I do not have a daughter,

I do not have a flower.

There are hundreds of villages,

Please go ask others for flowers.


MAN: You are hiding your daughter,

You are hiding your flower.

A pedlar from Jiangxi

Went to your house to sell needles and threads,

And found that

Your daughter loves needles and threads.

He saw your daughter,

And he told me

That you have a daughter.

He told me so.

Your daughter cannot be hidden anymore,

藏也藏不住，
你家小姑娘，
一定给我家。

女：你说得我心欢，
你说得我心乐。
我家有个女，
我家有朵花。
货郎来我家，
我家小姑娘，
爱针又爱线，
实在买了针，
实在买了线。
躲也躲不住，
藏也藏不住。
不给不好说，
我就答应给你家。

天上有云才下雨，
地下有媒才成亲，
要请媒人来，
上门来说亲。

男：姑娘给我家，
你家奶奶答应了，
你家老爹答应了，
明天就去找媒人，
请媒来说亲。

214

Your daughter cannot be hidden any longer.

Please agree to marry her

To my family.


WOMAN: Your words pleased me a lot,

Your words cheered my heart.

I do have a daughter,

I do have a flower.

The peddler did come to my house.

My daughter loves needles

And threads,

She did buy needles,

And threads.

She cannot be hidden anymore,

She cannot be hidden any longer.

I cannot refuse you anymore,

And I agree to marry her to your family.


Rain comes only with clouds,

Marriage accomplishes only with matchmakers.

You need to hire a matchmaker

To come to my house to perform.


MAN: You has agreed to marry your daughter to my family,

Grandma has agreed,

Grandpa has agreed,

I will get a matchmaker tomorrow

To go to your house to perform.

女：古时哪个先成亲？
哪个最先做媒人？
哪个跟着学媒人？

男：张仕、白花①先成亲，
梅树李树先做媒，
媒人向它学，
学它做媒人。

女：哪个月来说亲？
哪一天来说亲？
什么时候媒人到我家？

男：正月是头月，
初二日子好，
我请媒人来，
正月初三到你家。

女：说亲日子定好了。
哪月吃定酒？
哪日讨红庚？

男：二月初八日，
双月双日日子好，
讨红庚就在那一天。

---

① 张仕、白花男女二人都是单身，后来在梅树下相见成亲。

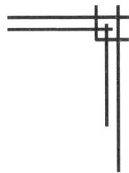

WOMAN: I want to ask you,

Who got married first in ancient times?

Who was the first matchmaker?

Who learned to be matchmaker afterwards?


MAN: Zhangshi and Baihua① got married first,

Plum trees were the first matchmakers,

People learned from them afterwards,

People learned to be matchmakers.


WOMAN: When will the matchmaker come to my house?

In which month?

On which day?


MAN: January is the first month of the new year,

And January second is a good day.

I will invite a matchmaker

To your house on January third.


WOMAN: The date for a matchmaker to come now is set,

In which month and on which day

Will we hold the engagement ceremony for the new couple?


MAN: February eighth is a good day,

Even numbers will bring us good luck,

We will hold the engagement ceremony on that day.

---

①　Names of two single young people, later, they became lovers.

女：拿什么来讨红庚？
你要说给我来听。

男：背着草烟来讨红庚，
背着猪膀来讨红庚，
背着定酒来讨红庚。

女：定酒背来了，
要请哪些人？

男：外公请来，
外婆请来，
舅舅请来，
舅妈请来，
姨妈请来，
姑爹请来，
奶奶请来，
老爹请来，
族中老小都请来。

客人请来了，
定酒吃过了，
我家一时讨不起，
说不定要等三年，
说不定要等五年。

女：我家小姑娘，
一天一天长大了，

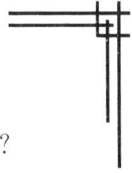

WOMAN: What will you bring as gifts for the ceremony?
Please let me know specifically.

MAN: I will bring tobacco,
I will bring pork shanks,
I will bring liquor and wine for the engagement ceremony.

WOMAN: Liquor and wine are set,
Who will you invite to attend the engagement ceremony?

MAN: I will invite grandpa from mother's side,
I will invite grandma from mother's side,
I will invite uncle from mother's side,
I will invite aunt from mother's side,
I will invite aunt from father's side,
I will invite uncle from father's side,
I will invite grandma from father's side,
I will invite grandpa from father's side,
People in the whole big family will be invited.

But after I treat all the guests,
And hold the engagement ceremony,
I am not be able to afford the wedding ceremony.
I need three or even five years
To save enough money for it.

WOMAN: My daughter is growing up
Day after day,

心也大起来了，
你家不讨不行了，
我家不嫁不行了。
择个好日子，
你家快快讨。

男：大年初二日子好，
讨亲就在那天讨。

女：大年初二日子好，
是走亲戚的日子，
不是讨亲的日子。

男：二月初九日子好，
讨亲就在那天讨。

女：二月初九日子好，
是平民百姓串会的日子，
不是讨亲的日子。

男：三月二十八，
讨亲就是那天好。

女：三月二十八，
是牟定城里赶街日，
不是讨亲的日子。

She will be more and more eager to go outside,

She will not wait for too long to marry,

You will need to set a date for marrying her soon.

Please select a good day,

And marry her shortly after.

MAN: January second is a good day,

We will hold the wedding ceremony on that day.

WOMAN: January second is a good day,

But it is a day for visiting relatives and offering new year greetings,

It is not a day for the wedding ceremony.

MAN: February ninth is a good day,

We will hold the wedding ceremony on that day.

WOMAN: February ninth is a good day,

But it is a day for visiting temple fairs,

It is not a day for holding the wedding ceremony.

MAN: March twenty-eighth is a good day.

We will hold the wedding ceremony on that day.

WOMAN: March twenty-eighth is a good day.

But it is a day for going to marketing fairs in Mouding City,

It is not a day for holding the wedding ceremony.

男：好不过四月初八那一天，
讨亲就在那天讨。

女：四月初八那一天，
是大官小吏科考日，
不是讨亲的日子。

男：五月初五日子好，
讨亲就在那天讨。

女：五月初五日子好，
是药王菩萨的生日，
不是讨亲的日子。

男：好不过六月二十四，
讨亲就在那天讨。

女：六月二十四虽然好，
是给田公地母烧香的日子，
不是讨亲的日子。

男：七月十四日子好，
讨亲就在那天讨。

女：七月十四日子好，
那天晚上要送祖，
不是讨亲的日子。

MAN: April eighth is a good day.

We will hold the wedding ceremony on that day.

WOMAN: April eighth is a good day.

But it is a day for imperial examination,

It is not a day for holding the wedding ceremony.

MAN: May fifth is a good day.

We will hold the wedding ceremony on that day.

WOMAN: May fifth is a good day.

But it is the birthday of Bodhisattva of Medicine,

It is not a day for holding the wedding ceremony.

MAN: June twenty-forth is a good day,

We will hold the wedding ceremony on that day.

WOMAN: June twenty-forth is a good day,

But it is a day for burning incense to Lord of Soil,

It is not a day for holding the wedding ceremony.

MAN: July fourteenth is a good day.

We will hold the wedding ceremony on that day.

WOMAN: July fourteenth is a good day,

But it is a day for worshiping ancestors at night,

It is not a day for holding the wedding ceremony.

男：好不过八月十五那一天，
讨亲就是那天好。

女：八月十五好倒好，
是月亮和太阳相遇的日子，
不是讨亲的日子。

男：九月初九日子好，
讨亲就在那天讨。

女：九月初九日子好，
是九星大会日，
不是讨亲的日子。

男：冬月头十天，
冬至那天好。

女：冬至日子好倒好，
那是皇帝老倌过年日，
大官小吏过节日，
不是讨亲的日子。

男：一年十二月，
腊月那月好。

MAN：August fifteenth is a good day.

We will hold the wedding ceremony on that day.


WOMAN：August fifteenth is a good day,

But it is a day when the sun meets the moon,

It is not a day for holding the wedding ceremony.


MAN：September ninth is a good day.

We will hold the wedding ceremony on that day.


WOMAN：September ninth is a good day,

But it is a day for the Nine Stars Meeting,

It is not a day for holding the wedding ceremony.


MAN：November tenth, the day of Winter Solstice①, is a
good day.

We will hold the wedding ceremony on that day.


WOMAN：The day of Winter Solstice is a good day,

But it is a day for emperors and officials

To celebrate the New Year,

It is not a day for holding the wedding ceremony.


MAN：There are twelve months in one year,

And December is a good month,

---

①　Winter Solstice, one term of the 24 Solar Terms, usually in the
early November on the lunar calendar.

一月三十天，
初八那天好。
腊月腊八日子到，
我家就来讨。

女：腊月腊八日子好，
我家喜欢了，
我家答应了。

男：日子择定了，
高山砍树枝，
搭起棚子来，
杀猪又宰羊，
酒席办起来。
四方客人都请到，
花衣花裙穿出来。
芦笙吹得响，
唢呐吹得响，
吹吹打打讨媳妇。

女：我家没吃的，
我家没穿的，
没吃没穿怎么嫁？

男：我家喂的三年大肥猪，
养的七年老绵羊。
肥猪宰一个，

There are thirty days in this month,

And the eighth day is a good day.

When the December eighth come,

We will hold the wedding ceremony.


WOMAN: December eighth is a good day,

We agree on the date,

You have our consent.


MAN: Now the date is set,

We are ready to go up to high mountains and cut tree branches

down,

So as to build a hut.

We will slaughter pigs and sheep

To host the feast.

We will invite the guests from around the country,

We will put on colorful clothes.

We will play the Lusheng loudly,

We will play the Suona loudly,

So as to welcome your daughter to marry to my family.


WOMAN: Our family does not have enough food to eat,

Our family does not have enough clothes to wear,

How will my daughter get married without food and clothes?


MAN: I have fat pigs that have been raised for three years,

I have old sheep that have been raised for seven years.

I will bring one pig,

绵羊拉一双，
好酒挑两罐，
新布拿三件，
环子打一双，
再挑一个小盒子。
挑进你家门，
亲亲热热送你家。

女：酒罐哪里歇？
小盒哪里放？
羊子哪里拴？

男：你家厦子下，
四方桌子摆起来，
小盒放中间，
两个酒罐摆两边。
你家厦子下，
绵羊拴在柱子上。

女：摆也摆好了，
拴也拴好了，
我要问问你，
小盒哪个做？
酒罐哪里来？

男：剑川木匠做小盒，
用楸木板做，
做得真是好；

I will bring two sheep,

I will bring two jars of fine liquor,

I will bring three bolts of brand-new cloth,

I will make a pair of earrings,

And have them set a gift box,

I will bring all of these things

To your house warmly and happily.


WOMAN: Where will you put your liquor jars?

Where will you put your gift box?

Where will you tie your sheep?


MAN: We will set a table

In the wooden hut,

We will put the gift box in the middle of the table,

We will put two jars on each side,

We will tie the sheep to a pol,

In the wooden hut.


WOMAN: Now there are places to put things

And to tie sheep.

I want to ask you,

Who will make the gift box?

Who will make the liquor jars?


MAN: Carpenters in Jianchuan will make gift boxs,

They make boxes from catalpa wood,

They have great craftsmanship.

直山直台人做酒罐，
用黄泥白泥做，
做得实在好。

女：小盒里头装什么？
酒罐里头装什么？
什么绳子拴小盒？
什么绳子拴酒罐？

男：小盒里头装着老肥肉，
酒罐里头装着好烧酒。
红色丝线拴小盒，
红色丝线拴酒罐。

女：小盒拴好了，
酒罐拴好了，
拴得又稳当，
拴得又好看。
哪个开小盒？
哪个开酒罐？

男：舅舅开小盒，
开出肥肉来待客。
外公外婆开酒罐，
外公开左边，
外婆开右边，
开出烧酒来待客。

People in Zhitai will make liquor jars,

They make jars from yellow and white clay,

They have great craftsmanship.


WOMAN: What will you put in the box?

What will you put in the jar?

What will you use to decorate the box?

What will you use to decorate the jar?


MAN: Fatty meat will be put in the box,

Good liquor will be put in the jar.

Red silk thread will be used to tie the box,

Red silk thread will be used to tie the jar.


WOMAN: When the box is ready,

Being set tight and stable.

When the jars are ready,

Being nice and beautiful.

Who will open the box?

Who will open the jars?


MAN: Uncle will open the box,

And bring the fatty meat out to entertain the guests.

Grandparents will open the jars,

Grandpa will open the one on the left,

Grandma will open the one on the right,

They will bring the liquor out to entertain the guests.

女：肉已开出来，
酒已开出来，
待客怎样待？
请你说给我。

男：桌子摆起来，
碗筷拿出来，
酒酒肉肉摆出来，
小菜端出来。
待客这样待，
恭恭敬敬地待。
客已待好了，
姑娘走得了。

女：我家新姑娘，
头上没包的，
身上没穿的，
脚上没穿的，
手上没戴的，
没穿没戴怎出嫁？

男：头上没包的，
给她青色包头布。
身上没穿的，
给她新衣裳。
脚上没穿的，
给她新花鞋。
手上没戴的，
金银手镯给她戴。

WOMAN：When the meat is ready,
And the liquor is ready,
What will you do to entertain the guests?
Please tell me.

MAN：I will set up a table,
And lay out bowls and chopsticks,
I will serve liquor and meat,
And as well as all dishes,
I will serve the guests
With great respect.
The guests will be fully satisfied,
And your daughter will be proud to get married.

WOMAN：My daughter is a bride,
But with no decorations to put on her head,
No new clothes to wear,
No new shoes to put on her feet,
No jewelry to wear,
How will she get married?

MAN：No decorations to put on her head?
Here is a blue headscarf for her.
No new clothes to wear?
Here are new clothes for her.
No new shoes to put on her feet?
Here are new shoes for her.
No jewelry to wear?
Here are gold and silver bracelets for her.

233

女：青色包头布，
包得真好看。
脚上新花鞋，
穿起也好看。
还要问问你：
新衣哪里来？

男：剑川人抽蚕丝，
剑川人纺丝线，
丝线织绸缎，
新衣做出来。

女：蚕丝抽好了，
丝线纺好了。
什么马来驮？
驮到哪里歇？

男：枣骝花马驮丝线，
花脚骡子驮丝线。
驮到昆明城，
城里歇两驮，
城外歇两驮，
城正中间歇两驮。

女：丝线驮来了，
驮来可要织？
要织又在哪里织？

WOMAN: The blue headscarf is beautiful,

And it is pretty to wear on one's head.

The new shoes are beautiful,

And they are pretty to wear on one's feet.

I want to ask you,

Where will you get new clothes?


MAN: Jianchuan people spin silk,

Jianchuan people weave silk thread.

They weave silk thread into silk satin,

And they make new clothes.


WOMAN: After spinning silk,

After weaving silk threads,

What horses will carry them on their backs?

Where will the horses go?


MAN: Horses with stripes on their bodies will carry the silk

thread,

Mules with stripes on their bodies will carry the silk threads.

They will carry the silk threads to Kunming City,

They will unload two packages in the centre of the city,

They will unload two packages outside the city,

And they will unload two packages in the city.


WOMAN: When the silk threads are ready,

Do they need to be woven?

Where do people weave them?

男：昆明城里街子上，
三层楼上头，
红栎麻栎做机床，
牛角做梭子，
黄竹做扣子，
织布就在那里织。

女：织去又织来，
织成什么布？

男：织去织来织成龙布，
织去织来织成蛇布；
织去织来织成绸子，
织去织来织成缎子；
织成绸缎做新衣，
新衣送给新娘穿。

女：你说织成龙布，
你说织成蛇布。
那是九皇大会上，
火神大将穿的衣，
不是新娘穿的衣。
你说织成绸子，
你说织成缎子，
那是大官小吏穿的衣，
不是新娘穿的衣。
实实说给你：
新娘穿的棉布衣。

MAN: In the street of Kunming City,

There is a loom in a building of three floors.

The loom frame is made of chestnut wood,

The loom shuttles are made of ox horns,

The loom beams are made of bamboo strips,

People will weave cloth there.


WOMAN: What kind of cloth will people weave?

What pattern will people weave?


MAN: People will weave dragon-patterned cloth,

People will weave snake-patterned cloth.

People will weave silk cloth,

People will weave satin cloth.

People will make new clothes,

People will make new clothes for the bride.


WOMAN: You said people will weave dragon-patterned cloth,

You said people will weave snake-patterned cloth,

But those are used for making clothes for deities,

To wear in the emperor general meetings,

Those clothes are not for the bride.

You said people will weave silk cloth,

You said people will weave satin cloth,

But those are used for making clothes for officials,

Those clothes are not for the bride.

I would like to tell you in specifics,

It is the cotton clothes that the bride will wear.

棉籽出在哪一点？
请你说给我来听。

男：耿马制定山，
有三个竹筒，
竹筒里面装棉籽，
棉籽就从那里来。

女：花籽找着了，
拿来哪里撒？

男：耿马制定山，
有三丘板田，
有三丘蒿子地，
那就是撒花的田，
那就是种花的地。

女：撒花田有了，
种花地有了，
没有撒花人，
没有种花人。

男：傣族人三个，
阿卡人三个，
就是撒花人，
就是种花人。

Where are the cotton seeds from?
Please tell me.

MAN: There are three bamboo tubes
On Mount Zhiding in Gengma①,
There are cotton seeds in these bamboo tubes,
That is where cotton seeds are from.

WOMAN: When finding those seeds,
Where will you sow them?

MAN: On Mount Zhiding in Gengma,
There are three areas of hardened lands,
These lands are covered by wormwood.
That is where people sow cotton seeds,
That is where people plant cotton seeds.

WOMAN: Now there are lands to sow cotton seeds,
Now there are lands to plant cotton seeds,
But there are no people to sow cotton seeds,
But there are no people to plant cotton seeds.

MAN: Find three Dai people,
Find three Aka② people.
They will sow cotton seeds,
They will plant cotton seeds.

---

① Gengma: name of a county in Yunnan Province.
② Aka: name of an ethnic group.

女：撒花人有了，
　　种花人有了，
　　什么节令撒花？
　　什么节令种花？

男：惊蛰撒头花，
　　清明撒二花，
　　立夏撒尾花。

女：春雨下三阵，
　　花籽出齐了。
　　什么人薅花？
　　什么人铲花？

男：傣族小姑娘，
　　拿着锄头来薅花，
　　拿着锄头来铲花。
　　薅也薅得好，
　　铲也铲得好。
　　秋雨下三阵，
　　花就长大了。

WOMAN: Now there are people to sow cotton seeds,

Now there are people to plant cotton seeds,

In which season will they sow cotton seeds?

In which season will they plant cotton seeds?


MAN: On the Waking of Insects① day, cotton seeds will be sowed.

On the Pure Brightness② day, cotton seeds will be sowed again.

On the Beginning of Summer③ day, cotton seeds will be sowed for the last time.


WOMAN: After three spring rain showers,

All seeds sprout.

Who will loosen the soil?

Who will fertilize the cotton fields?


MAN: Dai young ladies will loosen the soil with hoes,

Dai young ladies will fertilize the cotton fields with hoes.

They loosen the soil very well,

They fertilize the cotton fields very well.

After three autumn rain showers,

All cotton will be in full bloom.

---

① The Waking of Insects: one term of the 24 Solar Terms, refers to the springtime when spring storms wakes up all insects.

② Pure Brightness: one term of the 24 Solar Terms, usually in the mid springtime.

③ The Beginning of Summer: one term of the 24 Solar Terms.

女：哪月来采花？
哪日来采花？
哪个来采花？
用什么东西来装花？

男：九月霜降后，
就可采棉花；
傣族小姑娘，
采花就是她。
手里捏不下，
围腰里面兜，
围腰里面兜不下，
装在麻布口袋里头。

女：棉花拿到家，
什么地点来晒花？

男：房前屋后稻场上，
就是晒花的好地方。

女：花也晒干了，
花也晒好了，
花籽怎样隔？

男：编起黄竹大揽筛，
花籽一隔就隔开。

WOMAN: In which month will they pick cotton?

On which day will they pick cotton?

Who will pick cotton?

What will they use to carry cotton?

MAN: After the Frost's Descent① Day in September,

Cotton is ready to get picked.

Dai young ladies

Are ready to pick cotton.

When their hands cannot hold more cotton,

They use their aprons.

When their aprons cannot hold more cotton,

They use their sacks.

WOMAN: When cotton is taken home,

Where will people put it to dry in the sun?

MAN: The open ground around the house

Is perfect to put the cotton.

WOMAN: When cotton is dried

And completely dried,

How will people screen cotton seeds out?

MAN: A large sieve made of yellow bamboo splits will be used,

People will easily screen cotton seeds out.

---

① Frost's Descent: one term of the 24 Solar Terms, refers to the late autumn when it starts to frost in the early morning.

女：哪个来踩花？
哪个来称花？
哪个来装花？

男：傣族小姑娘来踩花，
傣族小伙子称花又装花。
满担一百二，
平担九十六，
棉花称好了，
麻布口袋装。

女：装也装好了，
什么马来驮？

男：枣骝滚蹄马，
紫毛玉顶马，
就是驮花马。

女：枣骝滚蹄马，
紫毛玉顶马，
是没兴头的马，
不是驮花马。

男：骒马枣骝马，
就是驮花马。

WOMAN: Who will tread the cotton?

Who will weigh the cotton?

Who will pack the cotton?

MAN: Dai young ladies will tread the cotton,

Dai young men will weigh and pack the cotton.

One full Dan① weighs sixty kilograms,

One flat Dan weighs forty-eight kilograms.

After weighing the cotton,

People use linen sacks to pack the cotton.

WOMAN: When people pack up the cotton,

What horse will carry them?

MAN: Horses with red fur and round hooves,

Horses with purple fur and white hair,

They are horses to carry the cotton.

WOMAN: Horses with red fur and round hooves,

Horses with purple fur and white hair,

They are not energetic horses,

They are not the right ones to carry the cotton.

MAN: Hinnys with red fur,

They are the right ones to carry the cotton.

---

① Dan is a carrying pole, and thus also used as a unit of weight for its loads. One Dan is 50 kilograms. A full Dan is usually a little more than one Dan; a flat Dan is usually a little less than one Dan.

女：骒马枣骝马，
是耪田种地收五谷的马，
不是驮花马。

男：小疙瘩骡子，
就是驮花马。

女：小疙瘩骡子，
是驮铜铁的马，
不是驮花马。

男：骡子四脚白，
骡子玉尾花，
身子就像花，
就是驮花马。
过街过得去，
驮到哪里都不费力气。

女：驮花可过街？
驮花可过关？
过街过关怎么过？

男：驮花要过街，
驮花要过关，
走过城里街，
驮子歇在街子上，
收税人走过来，

WOMAN: Hinnys with red fur,

They are good for farmwork,

But not the right ones to carry the cotton.


MAN: Those little mules,

They are the right ones to carry the cotton.


WOMAN: Those little mules,

They are good for carring the iron and copper,

But not the right ones to carry the cotton.


MAN: Mules' hooves are white,

Mules' tails are like flowers,

Mules' bodies are like flowers,

They are the right ones to carry the cotton.

They will carry the cotton and go through streets

With little efforts.


WOMAN: Will the mules carry the cotton and go through

streets?

Will they carry the cotton and go through barriers?

What will happen?


MAN: The mules will go through streets,

They will go through barriers.

When going through streets in town,

They will have a rest,

The tax collector will come over and stamp the seal,

大印盖三颗，
托子盖三颗。
过街这样过，
过关这样过。

女：哪个先买花？
请你说给我来听。

男：三个白族小姑娘，
戥子插在腰带上，
她们先买花。

女：买花买得了，
什么人弹花？
什么人纺花？
什么人纺线？
什么人织布？
请你说给我来听。

男：白族小伙子，
他们会弹花；
白族小姑娘，
她们会织布。

女：织布要机床，
什么材料做机床？
什么手艺做机床？

梅葛
Meige

248

He will stamp the seals three times

On those loads,

Therefore, the mules will go through streets,

They will go through barriers.


WOMAN: Who will buy the cotton first?

Please tell me.


MAN: Three Bai young ladies

With small scales carried in their belts,

They will buy the cotton first.


WOMAN: Now that people will buy the cotton,

Who will fluff the cotton?

Who will spin the cotton?

Who will spin the cotton into threads?

Who will weave the cotton threads into cloth?

Please tell me.


MAN: Bai young men

Know how to fluff the cotton,

Bai young girls

Know how to weave the cotton cloth.


WOMAN: People would need looms for weaving.

What to use to build looms?

What crafts to use to build looms?

男：织布要机床，
红栎麻栎做机床，
青冈栎树做床柱，
牛角做梭子，
黄竹做扣子。
张班做机床，
鲁班做纺架。

女：织去又织来，
织成什么布？

男：织去织来织成红布蓝布，
织去织来织成青布黄布。

女：大件有多长？
小件有多长？

男：大件四丈八，
小件二丈四。

女：大件小件织出来，
各种颜色都齐全，
新娘穿的倒有了。

MAN: Looms are needed for weaving cloth.

Chestnut wood is used to build loom frames,

Oak wood is used to build loom castles,

Ox horns are used to make shuttles,

Bamboo strips are used to make loom beams.

Master Zhang① 's craft will be used to build looms,

Master Lu's craft will be used to build looms.


WOMAN: After the weaving work,

What cloth will they make?


MAN: They will make red and blue cloth,

They will make blue and yellow cloth.


WOMAN: How long is a large bolt of cloth?

How long is a small bolt of cloth?


MAN: A large bolt of cloth is in the length of four Zhang and

eight Cun,

A small bolt of cloth is in the length of two Zhang and four

Cun.


WOMAN: Now that there are both large and small bolts of

cloth,

Now that there are various colors,

The bride would have clothes to wear.

---

① Both Zhang and Lu are family names.

金银首饰哪里来？
金银哪里出？
请你说给我来听。

男：金子出在金沙江，
银子出在银沙江。

女：哪个先晓得？
请你说给我来听。

男：湖广三女子，
金银她们先晓得。

女：湖广三女子，
她们怎样晓得的？

男：湖广女子养鹅，
湖广女子养鸭，
鹅鸭吃到金江银江去。
鹅用白嘴拣银子。
鸭用黄嘴拣金子，

女：什么是装金子的袋？
什么是装银子的袋？

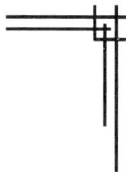

Where will people get gold and silver jewelry?

Where will people get gold and silver?

Please tell me.

MAN: Gold is from River Jinsha,

Silver is from River Yinsha.

WOMAN: Who came to know this first?

Please tell me.

MAN: Three women from Huguang Area①,

They came to know this first.

WOMAN: Three women from Huguang Area,

How did they get to know this first?

MAN: They raise geese,

They raise ducks,

When they herd geese and ducks to River Jinsha and River

Yinsha,

Geese pick out silver with their white bills,

Ducks pick out gold with their yellow bills.

WOMAN: What do people use to put gold in?

What do people use to put silver in?

---

① Huguang Area is in the Central China, referring to Hubei and
Hunan provinces with numerous lakes in particular.

男：鸭嗉子是装金袋，
鹅嗉子是装银袋。

女：什么人打金子？
什么人打银子？

男：湖广人打金子，
湖广人打银子。
打成金手箍，
打成银手箍，
打成金环子，
打成银环子。
你家新姑娘，
戴也戴齐了，
这回走得了！

女：我家新姑娘，
新衣新鞋穿好了，
金银首饰戴好了，
就是头上没有花，
你说怎么办？

男：正月给她戴朵门彩花，
二月给她戴朵龙头花。

254

MAN: Ducks' crops are packs to put gold in,
Geese's crops are packs to put silver in.

WOMAN: Who will forge gold?
Who will forge silver?

MAN: People from Huguang area will forge gold,
People from Huguang area will forge silver.
They will make gold bracelets,
They will make silver bracelets,
They will make gold rings,
They will make silver rings.
Now your daughter as the bride
Would has plenty of jewelry indeed.
She will get married happily.

WOMAN: Now my daughter has new clothes,
As well as new shoes,
Now my daughter has new jewelry,
But still has no flowers to wear on her head.
What will you do?

MAN: I will give her a Mencai flower ① to wear in January,
And a Longtou flower ② to wear in February.

---

①　The literal meaning of Mencai flower is colorful door flower.
②　The literal meaning of Longtou flower is dragon head flower.

女：正月门彩花，
是新年门上戴的花；
二月龙头花，
是菩萨戴的花，
不是新娘戴的花。

男：三月黄菜花，
四月小秧花，
就是新娘戴的花。

女：三月黄菜花，
是蜜蜂采的花；
四月小秧花，
是小秧戴的花，
不是新娘戴的花。

男：五月秧穗花，
六月纸香花，
就是新娘戴的花。

女：五月秧穗花，
是耪田种地时戴的花；
六月纸香花，

WOMAN：The Mencai flowers in January，

Are used to decorate doors during the Spring Festival.

The Longtou flowers in February，

Are flowers for bodhisattva to wear，

But not for the bride.


MAN：I will give her a Huangcai flower① in March，

And a Xiaoyang flower② in April.

They are flowers for the bride to wear.


WOMAN：The Huangcai flowers in March，

Are flowers for little bee to gather honey.

The Xiaoyang flowers in April，

Are young rice flowers，

They are not flowers for the bride to wear.


MAN：I will give her a Yangsui flower③ in May，

I will give her a Zhixiang flower④ in June.

They are flowers for the bride to wear.


WOMAN：The Yangsui flowers in May，

Are flowers for people to wear when doing farmwork.

The Zhixiang flowers in June，

---

① The literal meaning of Huangcai flower is yellow vegetables flower.

② The literal meaning of Xiaoyang flower is little seedling flower.

③ The literal meaning of Yangshui flower is ear of rice flower.

④ The literal meaning of Zhixiang flower is paper scent flower.

是田公地母戴的花，
不是新娘戴的花。

男：七月苦荞花，
八月朝阳花，
就是新娘戴的花。

女：七月苦荞花，
是五谷戴的花；
八月朝阳花，
是太阳月亮相会戴的花，
不是新娘戴的花。

男：九月开菊花，
十月剪刀花，
就是新娘戴的花。

女：九月开菊花，
是九皇大会花；
十月剪刀花，
是饥荒年的花，
不是新娘戴的花。

Are flowers for the Lord of Soil.

They are not flowers for the bride to wear.

MAN：I will give her a Kuqiao flower① in July,

I will give her a Zhaoyang flower② in August.

They are flowers for the bride to wear.

WOMAN：The Kuqiao flowers in July,

Are buckwheat blooms.

The Zhaoyang flowers in August,

Are flowers for the sun and the moon when dating.

They are not flowers for the bride to wear.

MAN：I will give her a chrysanthemum flower in September,

I will give her a Jiandao flower③ in October.

They are flowers for the bride to wear.

WOMAN：The chrysanthemum flowers in September,

Are flowers for the emperor's general meetings.

The Jiandao flowers in October,

Are flowers in the time of famine,

They are not flowers for the bride to wear.

---

① The literal meaning of Kuqiao flower is tartary buckwheat flower.

② The literal meaning of Zhaoyang flower is morning sun flower.

③ The literal meaning of Jiandao flower is scissors flower.

男：冬月硬子花，
腊月腊梅花，
就是新娘戴的花。

女：冬月硬子花，
腊月腊梅花，
头朵开空花，
后朵才结果，
不是新娘戴的花。

男：院子中间十盆花，
院子外边松头花，
就是新娘戴的花。

女：院子中间十盆花，
院子外边松头花，
是笔墨砚瓦花，
是手上拿的花，
不是新娘戴的花。

男：梁上八卦花，
就是新娘戴的花。

MAN: I will give her a Yingzi flower① in November,

I will give her a plum flower in December.

They are flowers for the bride to wear.


WOMAN: The Yingzi flowers in November,

The plum flowers in December,

Their first blossom bears no fruits,

They bear fruits only after their second blossom.

They are not flowers for the bride.


MAN: There are ten basins of flowers in the yard,

And there are Songtou flowers② outside the yard,

They are flowers for the bride.


WOMAN: Those ten basins of flowers in the yard,

And the Songtou flowers outside the yard,

They are Bimoyanwa flowers③,

They are flowers to hold in hands,

They are not flowers for the bride.


MAN: There are spider web flowers on the beams,

They are flowers for the bride.

---

① The literal meaning of Yingzi flower is hard flower.

② The literal meaning of Songtou flower is pine top flower.

③ The literal meaning of Bimoyanwa flower is brushes and ink-slabs
flower.

女：梁上八卦花，
是房屋戴的花，
不是新娘戴的花。

男：永北街子上，
有些开不败的花，
就是新娘戴的花。

女：永北街子上，
开不败的花，
是大官小吏吃酒吃茶的花，
不是新娘戴的花。

男：硬花①有三朵，
软花有三朵，
你家要挑哪样花？

女：硬花有三朵，
软花有三朵，
我家新姑娘，
要的是硬花。

男：硬花戴着头也亮，
软花戴着身也亮，
这回嫁得了！

————————

① 硬花：即金花、银花。

WOMAN: The spider web flowers on the beams,

Are flowers for the roof to wear,

They are not flowers for the bride.


MAN: In the Yongbei Street,

There are flowers that never fade.

They are flowers for the bride.


WOMAN: Those flowers in the Yongbei Street

That never fade,

Are flowers for the officials to admire when having tea or wine.

They are not flowers for the bride.


MAN: There are three gold flowers,

There are three silver flowers,

Which one do you like?


WOMAN: There are three gold flowers,

There are three silver flowers,

What my daughter prefers,

Are those gold flowers.


MAN: The gold flowers make your daughter more beautiful,

The silver flowers make your daughter more graceful,

Now your daughter is ready to get married happily.

女：嫁是要嫁了，
我家新姑娘，
脚还没有洗，
叫我怎样交给你？

男：赵州新瓦盆，
就是洗脚盆，
左边抹三下，
右边抹三下，
脚洗干净了，
花鞋也穿好了，
这下嫁得成了。

女：嫁是要嫁了，
新郎新娘的陪郎是哪个？

男：小伙小伴接新娘，
嫂嫂妹妹陪新娘，
接的陪的都来了，
这回嫁得成了。

女：房外有三对雀，
叽里叽里叫。
我家姑娘胆子小，
她不敢出来。

男：房外叽里声，
不是雀在叫，

WOMAN：My daughter is almost ready to get married now,

But this bride,

she has not cleaned her feet yet,

I will not turn her over to you yet.


MAN：The new basin made in Zhaozhou,

Is your daughter's feet-washing basin.

The left foot will be washed three times,

The right foot will be washed three times,

Then her feet will be cleaned.

Your daughter is ready to wear colorful shoes,

She is ready to get married happily.


WOMAN：She is ready to get married now,

But who are the groomsmen and the bridesmaids?


MAN：Those friends of the groom are groomsmen,

Those sisters of the groom are bridesmaids.

Now they are already here,

And your daughter will get married now.


WOMAN：There are three sparrow couples outside the house,

They chirp noisily.

My daughter is shy

And not ready to come out.


MAN：The chirps outside

Are not the sound made by sparrows,

是三对葫芦笙在收。
新娘不要怕，
快快走出来。

女：我家姑娘出嫁了，
做爹做妈的心不乐。

男：不怕不必怕，
不愁不要愁。
白米饭有三碗，
糯米饭有三碗，
红肉有三碗，
阿爹左边来，
阿妈右边来。
新娘张开嘴，
衔给阿爹两嘴，
装在袖里头；
衔给阿妈两嘴，
装在围腰头。
阿爹心也乐，
阿妈心也乐。

女：我家老奶年纪老，
孙女嫁出去，
没人来服侍，
要根拐棍来探路。

266

But the sound made by Hulusheng.

Tell your daughter not to be afraid,

Please come out to get married.


WOMAN: My daughter is going to get married,

But the parents are reluctant.


MAN: There is no need to be upset,

There is no need to be reluctant.

There are three bowls of white rice,

There are three bowls of sticky rice,

There are three bowls of red meat.

Bride's father, please come to the left side,

Bride's mother, please come to the right side.

Bride,

Please feed your father with some food,

And save some food in his sleeves.

Bride, please feed your mother with some food,

And save some food in her apron.

Now the father is happy.

Now the mother is happy.


WOMAN: Bride's grandma is old.

There would be no one to look after her,

If the granddaughter gets married.

Grandma needs a stick to help her to walk.

我家老爹年纪老，
要吃好东西，
猪心和猪肝，
要送老爹吃。

房后有山神，
要杀公鸡来酬谢，
山神答应了，
成亲才周到。

房下有畜神，
也要杀鸡谢，
畜神答应了，
成亲才有儿和女。
家堂香火旺，
也要杀鸡来酬谢。

这些事情办到了，
我家姑娘就嫁了。

男：大事办得到，
小事办得到，
事事都办到，
一样一样照着办，
样样都办好，
这回嫁得了。

Bride's grandpa is old,

He needs to eat nutritious food,

Pork heart and pork liver

Shall be served.


God of Mountain is enshrined in the back yard of the house.

You need to sacrifice a rooster to worship him.

Only when we get the blessing from him,

The marriage will be happy and successful.


God of Livestock is enshrined in the house,

You need to sacrifice a rooster to worship him.

Only when we get the blessing from him,

The new couple will be blessed of children.

Incense should be burnt continuously in the back yard of the

house,

Roosters should be sacrificed to express gratitude.


If you will do it all,

My daughter will get married happily.


MAN: Big tasks will be done,

Small tasks will be done,

Every task will be done one by one,

Every task will be properly finished,

Every task will be perfectly accomplished.

Now your daughter will get married happily.

女：嫁是要嫁了，
我家姑娘心不乐，
用什么来哄新娘？

男：白米饭拿来哄新娘，
羊膀子拿来哄新娘，
喜酒拿来哄新娘，
哄得新娘嘻嘻笑。

女：我家姑娘，
到了你家坐哪里？

男：自家院子头，
四方桌子上，
新娘坐那里。

女：坐倒坐下了，
哪个来喂喜酒？
哪个来背新娘？
背到哪里去？

男：媒人来喂喜酒，
孃孃①来背新娘，
背到喜棚头。

女：新亲②来到了，
没有住处怎么办？

---

① 孃孃：父亲的妹妹。
② 新亲：新娘家来的人。

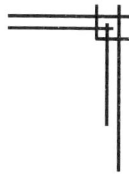

WOMAN: My daughter is ready to get married,

But she feels reluctant.

What will you do to cheer her up?

MAN: We will satisfy her with some white rice,

We will satisfy her with leg of lamb,

We will satisfy her with some wine.

We will definitely cheer her up.

WOMAN: When arriving at your house,

Where will my daughter sit?

MAN: She will sit on a square table,

Which is placed

In the middle of the yard.

WOMAN: When she sits down,

Who will serve her the wedding wine?

Who will carry her on their back?

Where will she be carried to?

MAN: The matchmaker will serve her the wedding wine,

Father's little sister will carry her on her back,

She will carry her to the shack for the wedding ceremony.

WOMAN: When the bride's family arrives,

Where will they stay?

男：房前三块玉米地，
房前三块菜籽地，
搭起棚子来，
盖起棚子来，
盖棚盖三格，
新亲住这里。

女：从前哪个先盖棚？
请你说给我来听。

男：欧梭莫梭人，
他们先盖棚。

女：先进棚子来，
抬头看天天补着，
低头看地地补着。
这是什么天？
这是什么地？

男：抬头看天天补着，
这是天底下的天，
树叶子做的天，
是讨亲嫁娶的天。
低头看地地补着，
这是地头上的地，
松毛做的地，
是讨亲嫁娶的地。

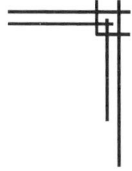

MAN: There are three corn fields in front of the house,
There are three rapeseed fields in front of the house.
Shacks will be built,
Shacks will be covered.
Shacks will be used
For the bride's families to stay.

WOMAN: Please tell me,
Who was the first to build shacks in ancient times?

MAN: It was the Ousuomosuo people,
They built shacks first.

WOMAN: When stepping into the shack,
Looking up, you will find the ceiling is broken,
Looking down, you will find the floor is broken.
What is wrong with the ceiling?
What is wrong with the floor?

MAN: The ceiling is not broken,
What you see
Is the tree leaves against the sky,
The ceiling is good for the wedding ceremony.
The floor is not broken,
What you see
Is the fallen pine needles on earth,
The floor is good for the wedding ceremony.

女：新亲有三百，
吃酒吃三天，
新亲坐下了，
你家待客怎样待？

男：三年装下好白米，
三年喂下老肥猪，
三年酿下好烧酒。
好酒好肉待客人，
恭恭敬敬待客人。

女：吃也吃完了，
吃也吃光了，
棚上的树叶晒干了，
棚下的松毛晒黄了。
对不起你家了，
姑娘交给你，
我们要散了。

男：三年装下的好白米，
还没有吃完；
三年喂下的老肥猪，
还没有吃完；
七年养下的大绵羊，
还没有吃完；
我要留住你，
吃的不好莫嫌弃。
昨天你交新娘，

WOMAN: The bride has three hundred family members,

They will stay for the wedding ceremony for three days.

How will you entertain them

When they arrive?


MAN: In the last three years, we have stored good white rice,

In the last three years, we have raised fat pigs,

In the last three years, we have made good wine.

We will serve all guests with good meat and wine,

We will entertain our guests with courtesy and respect.


WOMAN: Everyone finishes the meal,

Everyone enjoys the meal,

Tree leaves on the roof have dried in the sun,

Pine needles on the floor have dried in the sun.

We are sorry for bringing you troubles,

Now we will hand our daughter over to you,

We are heading back home.


MAN: The good white rice that we have stored for three years,

Is not eaten up yet.

The fat pigs that we have raised for three years,

Are not eaten up yet.

The fat sheep that we have raised for seven years,

Is not eaten up yet.

I hope that you are satisfied,

I hope that you will stay.

You handed your daughter over yesterday

新娘交给了媒人，
没有交给公婆。
今天你交新娘，
要交给公婆。
姑娘找不着活计做，
要你来安置。

女：妈的姑娘啊，
三月撒荞子，
五月去栽秧，
八月割谷子，
冬月种小麦，
你要忙着做。
推的拿到磨盘上，
舂的拿到碓盘上，
撮箕扫帚拿着去，
一年四季要这样做。
别人的爹妈是你的公婆，
公婆不准做的事，
你就千万别去做。
活计安置好了，
我们要回去了。

男：实在要回去，
我也没办法，
羊头羊蹄羊膀子猪脊膘，
搭起十二道桥，
把你送过去。

To the matchmaker,

But not the groom's parents.

Please hand your daughter over today

To the mother-in-law.

The bride does not know what chores to do,

Please teach her.


WOMAN: My dear daughter,

You will sow buckwheat seeds in March,

You will transplant seedlings in May,

You will reap crops in August,

You will grow wheat in November,

Those are the chores you will have to do.

You will use the mill stone,

You will use the pestle,

You will use the broom and dust collector,

Those are the tools you will have to use.

Your husband's parents are now your parents,

You will never do things

that are not allowed by them.

This is what I need to teach you,

Now it is time for us to leave.


MAN: If you really need to go,

I will not do anything else but to see you off.

I will build a special bridge

Made from organs of sheep and pig,

To send you back home.

女：十二道桥搭起来，
新亲要走了，
可有赶亲棍①?

男：五炷喜香一壶酒，
一只羊膀一块肉，
就是赶亲棍。

亲戚做好了，
两家哈哈笑。

## 三、请客②

娶亲了，
把客人请来了，
外公外婆来了，
舅妈姨妈来了
姑爹来了，
小伙子小姑娘来了，
族中老人都来了。

主：哪个带信来！
你才到我家。

---

① 赶亲棍：新亲要走时送的礼物。
② 这一节诗是彝族人民在喜庆的日子和节日宴会上唱的。

WOMAN: The bridge will be built,

The bride's family will head back,

Is a Ganqin Stick① ready for us?


MAN: There are five sticks of wedding incense and a pot of wine,

There is a leg of lamb and a hunk of meat,

This is the Ganqin Stick.


Now we become a big family officially,

Everyone is cheerful and happy.


## Section Three　Entertaining the Guests

When the wedding day came,

The guests came,

Grandparents from the bride's side came,

Aunts from the bride's side came,

Uncles from the bride's side came,

Young men and women came,

All the elders in the family came.


HOST: Who sent you the message,

And who brought you to my house?

---

① Ganqin Stick refers to the gifts for the bride's family when they go back home after the wedding ceremony.

客：什么是鸟王？
凤凰是鸟王。
凤凰带信来，
我才到你家。

主：凤凰只是飞过房头上，
没有带信到你家。

客：大雁带信来，
我才到你家。

主：大雁只从天上过，
没有带信到你家。

客：岩鸡带信来，
我才到你家。

主：岩鸡只从林中过，
没有带信到你家。

客：老鹰带信来，
我才到你家。

主：老鹰石岩上面飞，
没有带信到你家。

客：竹鸡箐鸡带信来，
我才到你家。

GUEST：What bird is the king of birds?
Phoenix is the king of birds.
A phoenix sent me the message,
And it brought me to your house.

HOST：Phoenix flew over your roof,
But it did not send any message to you.

GUEST：A wild goose sent me the message,
And it brought me to your house.

HOST：The wild goose only flew across the sky,
It did not bring any message to you.

GUEST：A wild rooster sent me the message,
And it brought me to your house.

HOST：The wild rooster only ran through the woods,
It did not bring any message to you.

GUEST：An eagle sent me the message,
And it brought me to your house.

HOST：The eagle only flew over the mountain rocks,
It did not bring any message to you.

GUEST：A bamboo rooster sent me the message,
And it brought me to your house.

主：竹鸡箐鸡箐里走，
没有带信到你家。

客：老鸹喜鹊带信来，
我才到你家。

主：老鸹只从房头过，
喜鹊只在门外飞，
没有带信到你家。

客：绿斑鸠带信来，
我才到你家。

主：绿斑鸠在荞地上头飞，
没有带信到你家。

客：画眉带信来，
我才到你家。

主：画眉从树下飞过去，
没有带信到你家。

客：布谷鸟带信来，
我才到你家。

主：布谷鸟分节令去了，
没有带信到你家。

HOST: The bamboo rooster only walked through the valleys,

It did not bring any message to you.

GUEST: A crow and a magpie sent me the message,

And they brought me to your house.

HOST: The crow only passed by your house,

The magpie only flew over your house,

They did not bring any message to you.

GUEST: A green turtledove sent me the message,

And it brought me to your house.

HOST: The green turtledove only flew over buckwheat fields,

It did not bring any message to you.

GUEST: A thrush brought me the message,

And it brought me to your house.

HOST: The thrush only flew through trees,

It did not bring any message to you.

GUEST: A cuckoo sent me the message,

And it brought me to your house.

HOST: The cuckoo was busy telling the world about the new season,

It did not bring any message to you.

客：鹦哥带信来，
我才到你家。

主：鹦哥在树上，
没有带信到你家。

客：飞天鸟带信来，
我才到你家。

主：飞天鸟到天王跟前缴粮去了，
到地王跟前缴粮去了，
没有带信到你家。

客：小蜜蜂带信来，
我才到你家。

主：小蜜蜂清早采露水去了。
没有带信到你家。

客：山兔子带信来，
我才到你家。

主：兔子只在山里跑，
没有带信到你家。

客：马鹿带信来，
我才到你家。

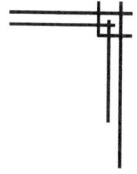

GUEST: A parrot sent me the message,
And it brought me to your house.

HOST: The parrot only rested in trees,
It did not bring any message to you.

GUEST: A skywards-flying bird sent me the message,
And it brought me to your house.

HOST: The skywards-flying bird was busy carrying grain
to Lords in heaven and lords on earth.
It did not bring any message to you.

GUEST: A little bee sent me the message,
And it brought me to your house.

HOST: The little bee went out in the early morning to find dew,
It did not bring any message to you.

GUEST: A wild rabbit sent me the message,
And it brought me to your house.

HOST: The wild rabbit only ran in the mountains,
It did not bring any message to you.

GUEST: A red deer sent me the message,
And it brought me to your house.

主：马鹿石岩边上跑，
没有带信到你家。

客：獐子麂子带信来，
我才到你家。

主：獐子被猎人捉去了，
麂子被猎人网去了，
没有带信到你家。

客：穿山甲带信来，
我才到你家。

主：穿山甲进洞去了，
没有带信到你家。

客：豪猪带信来，
我才到你家。

主：豪猪钻洞去了，
没有带信到你家。

客：狐狸带信来，
我才到你家。

主：狐狸偷吃的去了，
没有带信到你家。

HOST: The red deer only ran along the mountain rocks,
It did not bring any message to you.

GUEST: A river deer and a muntjac sent me the message,
And they brought me to your house.

HOST: The river deer was caught by hunters,
The muntjac was caught by hunters,
They did not bring any message to you.

GUEST: A pangolin sent me the message,
And it brought me to your house.

HOST: The pangolin only stayed in its hole,
It did not bring any message to you.

GUEST: A porcupine sent me the message,
And it brought me to your house.

HOST: The porcupine only stayed in its cave,
It did not bring any message to you.

GUEST: A fox sent me the message,
And it brought me to your house.

HOST: The fox went stealing food,
It did not bring any message to you.

客：石蚌带信来，
我才到你家。

主：石蚌在沟中洞里叫，
没有带信到你家。

客：白鱼带信来，
我才到你家。

主：白鱼水中游，
没有带信到你家。

客：地瓜根根带信来，
我才到你家。

主：地瓜根根确实带了信，
我们两家来认亲。

团团桌边坐，
喜喜欢欢来搳拳。
一样肉也没有，
一样酒也没有。
请把青菜当肉吃，
请把凉水当酒喝。

客：七十七样菜，
桌子摆得满满的。

GUEST：A stone clam sent me the message,

And it brought me to your house.

HOST：The stone clam stayed in its cave,

It did not bring any message to you.

GUEST：A white fish sent me the message,

And it brought me to your house.

HOST：The white fish only swam in water,

It did not bring any message to you.

GUEST：Roots of the sweet potato

Sent me the message,

And it brought me to your house.

HOST：Roots of the sweet potato did send my message,

You are indeed my guests.

We sit together,

And play games happily.

There is no meat,

There is no wine.

Please take vegetables as meat,

Please take water as wine.

GUEST：There are seventy-seven dishes,

And the table is fully piled with dishes.

土锅里面有好猪肉，

坛子里面有好白酒，

吃了好肉，

喝了好酒，

吃也吃饱了，

喝也喝够了，

吃了不再道谢啦，

喝了不再道谢啦。

# 四、抢棚①

主：抢棚的哥哥，

抢棚的妹妹，

我要问问你们，

我家娶亲你们怎么知道的？

客：春风吹三遍，

冬风刮三遍，

春风吹来我知道，

冬风刮来我知道，

我们爱玩爱跳，

有没有玩跳的地方？

---

① 抢棚：在新娘即将进门时，村里的青年男女就聚集在一起打
跳（跳舞），表示庆贺和欢乐。

There is delicious pork in the clay pot,

There is good liquor in the jar,

We have good meat,

We have good liquor.

We have a great meal,

We have a great drink,

Thank you for your dishes.

Thank you for your drinks.

# Section Four　Qiangpeng①

HOST: Young men who come to Qiangpeng,

Young women who come to Qiangpeng,

I want to ask you,

How do you know that there is a wedding ceremony in my family?

GUEST: The spring wind has blown three times,

The winter wind has blown three times,

The spring wind brought the message to us,

The winter wind brought the message to us,

We love to dance,

Shall we dance?

---

① A celebrating activity for young men and women to dance when welcoming the bride to the groom's house.

主：玩跳的地方倒有，
我要问问你们，
从前哪个先抢棚？
从前哪个先打跳？
你们可知道？

客：先抢棚的是李之成①，
先打跳的是李之成。

主：李之成在哪里打跳，
你们可知道？

客：李之成在南京城里打跳，
在皇帝老倌花园里打跳。
今晚你家娶亲，
我们爱玩，
我们爱跳。
玩跳的地点在哪里？

主：房前有三块玉米地，
有三块黄菜地，
玩跳的地点在那里。

_____

① 李之成：彝族民间故事《百雀衣》中的男主角。皇帝夺去了
他的妻子，他穿上百雀衣，吹着芦笙，装扮成一个惹人发笑的人到皇
宫打跳，用巧计杀死了皇帝。

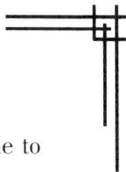

HOST：There is a wedding ceremony and you are welcome to dance,

But I want to ask you first,

Who was the first one to do Qiangpeng in ancient times?

Who was the first one to dance for celebrating?

Do you young people know?


GUEST：It was Li Zhicheng① who did Qiangpeng first,

It was Li Zhicheng who danced to celebrate first.


HOST：Will you tell me?

Where did Li dance?


GUEST：He danced in Nanjing City,

He danced in the garden of the palace.

There is a wedding ceremony in your home,

We love to dance,

We love to celebrate,

Where will we perform Qiangpeng?


HOST：There are three corn fields in front of the house,

There are three cabbage fields in front of the house,

You will dance there.

---

① Li zhicheng：name of a man, the hero in a folktale called *A Dress Made of the Feathers of One Hundred Peacocks*. In this folktale, the emperor took his wife away. Dressing up as a jester, he went dancing in the palace and killed the emperor by maneuver.

玩跳时怎样装扮？
头上戴什么？
身上穿什么？

客：大理草帽头上戴，
绣球结起来，
雉鸡尾插起来，
红绿花衣身上穿，
麻布花鞋穿起来。
我们这样装扮，
我们爱玩爱跳，
你家喜欢不喜欢？

主：我家也爱玩，
我家也爱跳，
怎么不喜欢。
听见一个声音，
不像人的声音，
不像鸟的声音，
那是什么声音？

客：那是葫芦笙，
葫芦笙吹起来，
玩也玩得成，
跳也跳得成。

主：葫芦笙是怎样做成的，
你们可知道？

What will you wear when dancing?

What will you put on your heads?

What clothes will you wear?

GUEST: We will put on straw hats made in Dali,

We will decorate the hats with embroidered balls,

We will decorate the hats with feather of pheasants,

We will put on red and green clothes,

We will put on colorful linen shoes.

We usually wear these.

We love dancing and celebrating.

Does your family like it?

HOST: Our family loves dancing,

Our family loves celebrating,

We certainly like it.

Do you hear some sounds?

It is not sounds made by human beings,

It is not sounds made by birds,

What sound is that?

GUEST: It is the sounds made by Hulusheng,

When it is played,

Everyone will dance,

Everyone will celebrate.

HOST: How is Hulusheng made?

Will you tell me?

客：葫芦配竹子，
做成葫芦笙。

主：哪里来的葫芦种？
哪里来的竹子种？

客：从前哥哥捉野鸡，
野鸡没捉到，
捉到一只小白兔。
划开兔子头，
葫芦种在里面，
竹子种也在里面。

主：哪个种葫芦？
哪个种竹子？

客：阿省莫若，
阿底莫若，
他俩种葫芦，
他俩种竹子。

主：葫芦笙做成了，
用什么来做葫芦心？

客：竹子削成响舌子，
就是葫芦心。

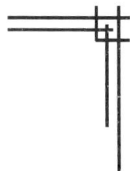

GUEST: Hulusheng is made from gourd and bamboo,
That's how it is made.

HOST: Where did people get gourd seeds?
Where did people get bamboo seeds?

GUEST: A long time ago,
There was a young man who went hunting for pheasants,
He ended up with only a little rabbit as prey.
He cut the rabbit's head open,
And found gourd seeds
And bamboo seeds inside.

HOST: Who sowed the gourd seeds?
Who sowed the bamboo seeds?

GUEST: Ashengmoruo did it,
Adimoruo① did it,
They planted gourds together,
They planted bamboo together.

HOST: Hulusheng was made,
Then what was used inside to make its heart?

GUEST: Bamboo chips were cut into whistles,
These were used to make the heart of Hulusheng.

① Both Ashengmoruo and Adimoruo are names of young men.

主：响舌做成葫芦心，
为何吹起没声音？

客：黄蜡拿一团，
糊起响舌子，
吹起有声音，
吹起响又响。

主：你们爱玩爱跳，
左边转还是右边转，
你们可知道？

客：左边转三转，
接着右边转，
脚要使力跳，
嘴要使劲吹，
我们玩跳到天亮。

## 五、撒种①

女：你我亲，
十年不办婚，
五年不办婚，
今年才办婚。

_____

① 撒种：在讨了媳妇的第二天清早唱的一段。用二人扮牛，在棚子里犁地撒种（男的代表新郎家，女的代表新娘家）。

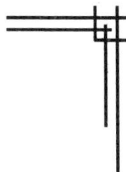

HOST: A bamboo whistle was made,

How to produce any sound?

GUEST: People took some yellow wax,

And paste it on whistle's heart,

The whistle then started to produce sounds,

Well and loud.

HOST: You love dancing,

But do you know,

When to make left or right turns?

GUEST: We will make a left turn three times,

And then a right turn instead.

Dancing hard with feet,

Blowing hard with mouth,

We will dance until dawn.

# Section Five　Seed-sowing①

WOMAN: We have been in love,

For ten years,

For five years,

But have not held the wedding ceremony until this year.

---

① It refers to a wedding tradition. In the next morning of the wedding day, one man from the groom's family and one woman from the bride's family will pretend to be bulls plowing the fields.

办婚可赶过年，
办婚可赶过月，
办婚可赶过日？

男：你我亲，
今年才办婚。
赶年赶过了，
赶月赶过了，
赶日赶过了。
赶年赶好年，
赶月赶好月，
赶日赶好日。
今天就是好日子，
婚事办起来。

天亮早早起，
棚子下边犁地又撒种。
犁牛头上没有角，
犁牛脚上没有蹄，
这不是真犁牛，
是办婚事的犁牛。

女：头上没有角，
脚上没有蹄，
这种犁牛哪里出？

男：南京应天府，
大坝柳树弯，

Did we choose this year?

Did we choose this month?

Did we choose this day?

MAN: We have been in love,

And have not held the wedding ceremony until this year.

We have chosen this year,

We have chosen this month,

We have chosen this day.

We have chosen a good year,

We have chosen a good month,

We have chosen a good day.

Today is a good day,

It is perfect for holding the wedding ceremony.


There are bulls plowing the fields

Early in the morning.

These bulls have no horns,

These bulls have no hooves.

They are not real bulls,

They are bulls for the wedding ceremony.


WOMAN: These bulls have no horns,

These bulls have no hooves,

Where are the bulls from?


MAN: In Nanjing Yingtianfu,

There is a crooked willow tree nearby a dam,

办婚事用的犁牛，
出在那地方。

女：牛在哪里架？
牛用什么喂？

男：家堂面前架双牛，
点起香来烧起纸，
白米肥肉当牛草，
高粱酒当牛水。

女：什么人吆牛？
怎样来装扮？

男：小伙子吆牛，
锄头倒扛着，
篮子倒背着；
倒扛锄头装扮肩膀，
倒背篮子装扮身子，
头发帽子装扮头。

女：牛也吆来了，
这回撒种了。
籽种哪里来？
哪个来撒种？

男：南山雪脉山，
籽种那里来。

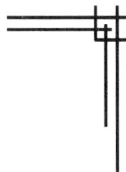

The bulls for the wedding ceremony
Are from there.

WOMAN: Where will the bulls be set?
What will the bulls be fed?

MAN: The bulls will be set in the hall centre of the house,
Incense and paper will be burned to worship them.
Rice and meat will be served as feeding grass,
Sorghum liquor will be served as feeding water.

WOMAN: Who will guide the bulls?
How will they be dressed?

MAN: A young man will carry two hoes upside down,
Pretending to be the shoulders of the bull.
He will carry one basket upside down,
Pretending to be the body of the bull.
He will wear a hat on his head,
Pretending to be the head of the bull.

WOMAN: The bulls are well set,
Then it is time to sow seeds.
Where do seeds come from?
Who will sow them?

MAN: From the snowy ridges in South Mountains,
Did the seeds come.

媒婆背籽种,
媒人撒种子:
甜荞羼大麦,
苦荞羼小麦,
黑豆羼红豆,
谷子羼豌豆,
五谷撒得满满的。

女：五谷撒满了,
转来要放牛,
放牛哪里放？

男：到了家堂前,
喜香烧起来,
黄纸开起来,
牛在那里放。

女：牛也放好了,
吆回哪一方？

男：南京应天府,
大坝柳树弯,
吆回那一方。

# 六、葫芦笙

彝家出了两个人,
一个叫阿省莫若,

The matchmaker will carry the seeds,

The matchmaker will sow the seeds.

Sweet buckwheat is mixed with wheat,

Bitter buckwheat is mixed with barley,

Black beans are mixed with red beans,

Millet is mixed with green beans,

All kinds of seeds are fully sowed.

WOMAN: Seeds are all sowed,

Will you set the bulls next?

Where will you set the bulls?

MAN: In the central hall,

We will burn the wedding incense,

We will supply yellow joss paper,

The bulls will be set there.

WOMAN: The bulls are well set,

Where will you head them to next?

MAN: In Nanjing Yingtianfu,

There is a crooked willow tree nearby a dam,

The bulls will be headed back there.

## Section Six　Hulusheng

There were two young men among Yi people,

One was called Ashengmoruo,

一个叫阿底莫若。
他俩有竹子种，
他俩有葫芦种。

阿省莫若拿着竹子种，
来到东洋大海沙滩上，
正当雷公发脾气，
雷声隆隆忙撒种。

正月二十属鼠日，
属鼠那天撒竹种，
竹子出得真是好。

四月二十日，
竹种撒下三个月，
阿省莫若走来看，
竹子长成节。

到了移植时，
选择一个好日子，
恰在五月端午节，
阿底莫若去栽竹。

石岩底下栽竹子，
长到石岩上面来，
竹子头被虫吃了。
去到树林里，

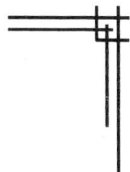

One was called Adimoruo.

They had bamboo seeds,

They had gourd seeds.

Ashengmoruo took bamboo seeds,

And went to the beach of the Eastern Sea.

During the time God of Thunder struck the sky,

He sowed seeds quickly under thunder and rain.

January twentieth was a day of the mouse,

It was a perfect day for sowing bamboo seeds.

Bamboo sprouted very well.

Three months after the sowing day,

On April twentieth,

Ashengmoruo came to check,

And found that bamboo seeds have grown into seedlings already.

It was time to set bamboo seedlings out,

They chose May fifth, the day of the Dragon Boat Festival,

It was a good day.

Adimoruo went to plant bamboo seedlings on that day.

Bamboo seedlings was planted by rocks.

When bamboo grew higher than rocks,

Its top was eaten by worms.

Adimoruo went to the woods,

请来啄木鸟。
啄木鸟医竹子，
竹子医好了。

哪个种葫芦？
傣族种葫芦。
二月二十属羊日，
属羊那天种，
葫芦长得好，
葫芦花好像棉花一个样。

竹子长大了，
葫芦长好了。
竹子砍成节，
葫芦挖个洞。
竹片做舌头，
放进竹节里。
竹节安在葫芦上，
公配母来母配子，
五个竹节各有音。
葫芦配竹节，
做成葫芦笙。

哪个做成的葫芦笙？
傣族做成的葫芦笙。
什么人来吹？
傣族人来吹。

And invited woodpeckers.

Woodpeckers ate the worms,

And the bamboo was saved.


Who planted gourds?

Dai people planted gourds.

They planted gourds

On February twentieth, the day of the sheep.

The gourds grew very well,

Their flowers looked like cotton.


Bamboo grew already,

Gourds grew already.

They cut bamboo into sections,

They poked holes in the gourds,

They used bamboo chips as tongues,

They set tongues into bamboo tubes,

They set bamboo tubes on the gourds.

All pieces matched well,

All five tubes could produce sounds.

They set gourds and bamboo tubes together,

They successfully made a Hulusheng.


Who created Hulusheng?

Dai people created it.

Who played Hulusheng?

Dai people played it.

竹节烙洞洞，
笛子做出来。
竹子削去皮，
响篾做出来。

响篾胸前挂，
笛子腰上插，
做时不爱人，
吹起爱死人。

男在高山吹笛子，
女在箐底吹树叶；
男在高山唱，
女在箐底来回音；
女在箐底唱，
男在高山来回音。

刀子石上磨，
伙伴唤拢来。
石头不会动，
调子能吹合，
唱得合心意，
绕着来相会。

好吃的是猪肉，
好喝的是白酒。
白米人人爱，

Little holes were poked on the bamboo tube,

This was how a flute was made.

Bamboo skin was peeled,

This was how a xiangmie was made.

Dai people hung xiangmie on their necks,

and put flutes under their belts.

Dai people did not like making mies and flutes,

But they loved playing them.

Man played the flute on top of the mountain,

Woman whistled back with a leaf down the valley.

Man sang on top of the mountain,

Woman echoed back down the valley.

Woman sang down the valley,

Man echoed back on top of the mountain.

The couple gathered together,

And sharpened knives on stones.

Stones would always stay in the way,

But the couple would bypass them to meet.

Their cheerful music matched,

Their beautiful tunes made harmony together.

Pork was scrumptious,

Liquor was tasty,

Rice was delicious,

哪个不爱玩，
玩了吹了回家来。

女的不好过，
以为是害伤风病。
不是伤风病，
有了身孕了。
怀了九个月，
娃娃就要生下来。

住在哪间屋里？
住在堂屋里。
堂屋里面有老人，
堂屋里面不能生娃娃。

住在哪间房里？
住在灶房里。
灶房里面有兄妹，
灶房里面不能生娃娃。

住在楼上房间里，
楼上是装谷米粮食的地方，
楼上不能生娃娃。

搬到西边厢房里，
叔伯大人望得见，
厢房里不能生娃娃。

They enjoyed everything,

And afterwards they went back home.

The woman felt sick,

Believing that she caught a cold.

She did not catch a cold,

She in fact got pregnant.

After nine months,

Her baby was due.

Which room would the woman stay in?

How about in the central hall?

Elders were living in the central hall,

She was not supposed to give birth there.

Which room would the woman stay in?

How about in the kitchen room?

Brothers and sisters were living in the kitchen room,

She was not supposed to give birth there.

Could the woman stay in the room upstairs?

It was a room for storing grain,

She was not supposed to give birth there.

How about the west chamber?

Uncles were living there and could see the room through,

She was not supposed to give birth there.

搬到内屋里面住，
才把娃娃生下来。

哪个剪脐带？
祖母剪脐带。
脐带剪断了，
娃娃包在围腰里，
要来洗娃娃。

没有清水洗，
跑到池塘边，
池塘清水鱼游过，
鱼游过的水不能洗娃娃。

又往大河跑，
跑到大河边，
只见浑水淌，
浑水不能洗娃娃。

又往箐里跑，
箐里有井水，
井水牛吃过，
牛吃过的水不能洗娃娃

又往岩石下面跑，
岩石下面有泉水，
泉水铜铁气味大，
这样的水不能洗娃娃。

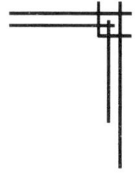

The woman moved to the inner chamber,

And finally gave birth there.


Who would cut baby's umbilical cord?

Grandma would do it.

After cutting it,

Grandma wrapped the baby with a piece of cloth,

Then it was time to bathe the baby.


There was no clean water,

They went to a pool for water.

There were fish swimming in the pool,

It was not proper to bathe the baby in this pool.


They went to a river

To see if the water was good,

There was only muddy water in the river,

It was not healthy to bathe the baby there.


They went to the valley for water,

And found a well.

Cattle drank water from this well,

It was not safe to bathe the baby there.


They went to the mountain rocks,

And found spring water underneath.

There was a strong smell of iron and cooper,

It was not safe to bathe the baby in the spring water.

又往林中跑，
林中有清水，
清水百鸟来喝过，
百鸟喝过的水不能洗娃娃。

到处跑遍了，
只得跑回来，
房后马缨花树下，
马缨树下清水流，
流水挑来洗娃娃，
娃娃就像马缨花。

新街买的锅，
冷水煨涨了，
好好洗娃娃，
娃娃长大逗人爱。
什么做洗槽？
马缨花树做洗槽。
什么陪伴洗？
马缨花儿陪伴洗。
中和的麻布做衣裳，
白井的棉布做裤子。

生下三天后，
就要取名字。

They went to the deep woods,

And found clean streams.

Birds had water from the streams,

It was not healthy to bathe the baby there.


They went everywhere,

But came back home in vain.

Under a Mayinghua tree in the back yard,

There was a clean stream.

The clean stream water was good for bathing the baby,

After taking a bath, the baby would be as lovely as a
Mayinghua flower.


They bought a new pot from Xinjie Street,

And warmed stream water up,

The baby was given a gentle and careful bath,

And looked very cute afterwards.

What was used as a sink?

A Mayinghua trunk was the sink.

Who was baby's companion while taking the bath?

Mayinghua flowers accompanied him.

Linen cloth from Zhonghe① was used to make clothes,

Cotton cloth from Baijing② was used to make pants.


Three days after birth,

The baby would be named.

---

① Zhonghe: name of a region.
② Baijing: name of a region.

松树林中取名字，
荞子花中取名字，
泉水边上取名字，
升斗当中取名字。
杀了一只红公鸡，
公鸡来祭树，
公鸡来祭水。
祭完大家吃，
吃了长辈取名字，
名字取出来，
指望娃娃快长大。

# 七、安家

两个娃娃会坐了，
两双小手一样长；
两个娃娃会站了，
站着个子一样高。

小哥小妹一处玩，
小哥玩白土，
小妹玩黄土，
白土当白饭，
黄土当黄饭。
烂瓦做小锅，

He could be named after pine woods,

He could be named after buckwheat flowers,

He could be named after streams,

He could be named after Sheng and Dou①.

A red rooster was offered as a sacrifice,

To worship the trees,

To worship the water,

People shared the red rooster after the worshipping ceremony,

The elders then named the baby officially.

The baby was named,

And he was blessed to grow up healthily.

## Section Seven    Settling Down

Two babies together learned how to sit,

Their hands were of the same length.

Two babies together learned how to stand,

They were of the same height.


Two little kids always played together,

Little boy played with white mud,

Little girl played with yellow mud.

They took white mud as white rice,

They took yellow mud as yellow rice.

They took broken tiles as pots,

---

①　Both Sheng and Dou are measurement tools

切肉切两块，
一块小哥吃，
一块小妹吃。
舀饭舀两碗，
一碗小哥吃，
一碗小妹吃。
我们两个啊，
要永远相好。

小妹做什么，
小哥跟着做。
耪田哥妹一起去，
放牛放羊一起去。

小妹走哪条路，
小哥跟着走。
脚迹合脚迹，
甩手一个样。

把羊放到山坡上，
扯把树叶垫着坐。
坐过的树叶，
永远留在山坡上。

耪田去到大河边，
搬块石头垫着坐。
坐过的石头，
永远留在大河边。

They cut meat into two pieces,
One for the boy,
One for the girl.
They made two bowls of rice,
One for the boy,
One for the girl,
The boy and girl said,
We would be together forever.

The boy followed the girl in doing things.
They went together
To plow the fields,
To herd sheep and cattle.

The boy followed the path the girl had taken.
Their tracks,
Their gestures,
Were always exactly the same.

When herding sheep on a mountain slope,
They sat on leaves,
And left those leaves
Forever on those spots.

When plowing fields near a river,
They sat on a big boulder,
And left that boulder
Forever by the river.

321

用米来煮饭，
生米会煮烂。
哥妹情意好，
永远不分散。

被窝里子白布做，
被窝面子青布做，
白布青布会盖烂，
哥妹的心永不变。

男：对面望妹家，
房子真是矮，
走起路来实在长，
你家的地方住得远。
有了情妹在，
不嫌路遥远。
小哥来到妹门前，
房前"噢啊"喊三声，
房后"噢啊"喊三声，
打过口哨吹笛子，
小妹可听见。

女：听是听见了，
就是出不来，
跑到大门边，
一口唾沫吐出来①，
小哥可听见。

----

① 这里吐唾沫是相约的暗号，并无厌弃之意。

When rice was cooked in a pot,

It would be easily boiled and spoiled.

The boy and girl loved each other,

And their love would never be spoiled.


The inner layer of a quilt was made of white cloth,

The outer layer of a quilt was made of blue cloth.

The layers would be worn out and torn someday,

But the boy and girl's love would never change.


MAN: When I saw your house from distance,

It looked so small.

When I walked all the way over to your house,

The road seemed endless.

I did not mind the distance at all,

I was so eager to see you.

When arriving at your house,

I called "o-a" three times in front of the house,

I called "o-a" three times in back of the house,

I played the flute and I whistled,

Did you hear me?


Woman: Of course I heard it,

But I could not go out,

I came close to the door,

And spat① to make a sound,

Did you hear me?

---

① A secret signal of date. There is no negative meaning.

男：听是听见了，
小妹家里有爹娘，
小妹家里养着狗，
小哥不敢进你家。

羊羔"咩咩"叫，
你没有说不喜欢的话，
母牛"哞哞"叫，
你真的答应了？
母鸡领小鸡，
小哥要领妹，
小妹啊！
你能不能自己做主？

女：小哥啊！
我爹把我嫁了，
我妈把我嫁了，
我两个都不晓得，
我两个都不知道。

我爹我妈说：
"天上黑云嫁白云，
天上绿云嫁黄云，
七星姊妹嫁星星，
天亮星嫁过天星，
天虹嫁地虹，
爹妈的女儿也得嫁。

MAN：Of course I heard it,

But I could not go into your house.

Your parents were at home,

Your dog was guarding the door.


The lamb was making em sounds,

The cow was making ah sounds,

You did not say any words,

Did you really give them a permission?

Hen wanted to take little chickens,

I wanted to take you,

Oh! My lady!

Did you really have the right to make a decision?


WOMAN：Oh! My man!

My father promised to marry me to someone else,

My mother promised to marry me to someone else,

I did not know that,

You did not know that.


My parents said,

"Black cloud marries white cloud,

Green cloud marries yellow cloud,

Seven-star sisters marries stars,

Bright star marries sky star,

Rainbow in sky marries rainbow on earth,

Our daughter will get married too.

"天上的龙要出嫁，
龙冠亮闪闪，
龙尾摆又摆。
背阴林里八哥也要嫁，
乌鸦嫁老鹰，
鹧鸪嫁斑鸠，
野鸡嫁竹鸡，
野鸭嫁雁鹅，
禽鸟嫁禽鸟，
爹妈的女儿也得嫁。

"豹子嫁给老虎，
老熊嫁给野猪，
黄鼠狼嫁麂子，
香獐嫁狐狸，
松鼠嫁白鼠，
恶狗嫁白狼，
爹妈的女儿也得嫁。

"黑水嫁白水，
波浪嫁暴风，
急水嫁弯河，
爹妈的女儿也得嫁。

"小水嫁大水，
绿水嫁红水，

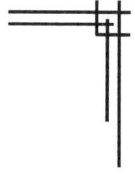

"Dragon in heaven gets married,

With its crown shinning,

And with its tail waving.

Mynah birds in deep woods get married,

Crows marry eagles,

Partridges marry turtledoves,

Pheasants marry bamboo chickens,

Wild ducks marry geese,

Birds marry birds,

Our daughter will get married too.

"Leopards marry tigers,

Bears marry boars,

Weasel marry muntjacs,

Musk deer marry foxes,

Squirrels marry white mouses,

Fierce dogs marry white wolves,

Our daughter will get married too.

"Black water marries white water,

Waves marry gales,

Rushing streams marry curving rivers,

Our daughter will get married too.

"Small streams marry big streams,

Green streams marry red streams,

慢水嫁快水，
爹妈的女儿也得嫁。

"黑鱼嫁白鱼，
蜻蜓嫁黑蛇，
白蚁嫁黑蚁，
爹妈的女儿也得嫁。

"银葫芦蜂嫁金葫芦蜂，
家蜂嫁土蜂，
苍蝇嫁毛虫，
爹妈的女儿也得嫁。

"大金蝴蝶要出嫁，
红花蝴蝶要出嫁，
金头蜻蜓要出嫁，
爹妈的女儿也得嫁。

"双尾虫虫要出嫁，
单尾虫虫要出嫁，
多脚虫虫要出嫁，
独脚虫虫要出嫁，
爹妈的女儿也得嫁。

"世间的虫虫都要出嫁，
世间万物都要出嫁，
爹妈的女儿也得嫁。

Slow streams marry quick streams,
Our daughter will get married too.

"Black fish marry white fish,
Dragonflies marry black snakes,
White ants marry black ants,
Our daughter will get married too.

"Silver bumblebees marry gold bumblebees,
Domestic bees marry wild bees,
Flies marry worms,
Our daughter will get married too.

"Big gold butterflies will get married,
Red butterflies will get married,
Gold dragonflies will get married,
Our daughter will get married too.

"Two-tailed worms will get married,
Single-tailed worms will get married,
Multi-footed worms will get married,
Single-footed worms will get married,
Our daughter will get married too.

"Every insect in the world will get married,
Every creature in the world will get married,
Our daughter will get married too.

"岩上'伯幺'①有三对，
河坝'山灵'②有二对，
人人见了都喊打。
要是我的女儿，
像'伯幺'一样，
像'山灵'一样，
她就别想活在世上。"

自从那天和你相会后，
找柴煮饭别人做，
我被关在屋子里，
太阳没有晒过我的脸，
太阳没有晒过我的脚，
我的小哥啊！
快快替我出主意。

男：小妹啊！
只要你愿意，
我来想办法，
我去捉麂子，
我去捉狐狸，
把兽肉送给你爹妈，
小哥用真心，
小哥用金银，
小哥一定要赎你。

---

① 伯幺：系昆虫，性淫。
② 山灵：系昆虫，性淫。

"There were three pairs of Boyao① on rocks,

There were two pairs of Shanling② on the riverbanks,

People all dislike them.

If my daughter,

Behaves like Boayo,

Behaves like Shanling,

She should die immediately."


After dating you on that day,

My parents locked me in the house,

And did not let me look for firewood and cook meals.

My face has not felt the sunshine from that time on,

My feet have not seen the sunshine from that time on,

Oh! My man!

Did you come to help me?


MAN: Oh! My lady!

I definitely did things for you,

If it could satisfy you.

I caught a muntjac,

I caught a fox,

I brought them to your parents.

I showed them my true heart,

I sent them my gold and silver,

I wanted to bail you out.

---

①　Boyao: a kind of lascivious insect.
②　Shanling: a kind of lascivious insect.

你的婆家来说亲，
费了三杯酒，
我还他三坛。
费了三块羊肉，
我还他三只羊。
费了三升米，
我还他三斗米。

你爹妈接了三钱金子，
我还他三两。
你爹妈接了五钱银子，
我还他五两。

接了三钱还三两，
接了五钱还五两。
戥子旺旺地称，
戥尾翘上天地称。

你婆婆心喜欢，
你婆婆心快乐，
我们两个就能成一家。

The family which intended to marry you

Sent you three cups of liquor,

I gave three jars back to them.

That family sent you three hunks of lamb,

I gave three whole sheep back to them.

That family sent you three Sheng① of rice,

I gave three Dou② back to them.


That family gave your parents three Qian③ of gold,

I gave three taels④ back to them.

That family gave your parents five Qian of gold,

I gave five taels back to them.


I spent three taels to pay his three Qian,

I spent five taels to pay his five Qian.

I measured the money with generosity,

I piled on the scale with money much more than needed.


Your parents would surely be satisfied,

Your parents would permit us

To get married.

---

①　Sheng：a monetary and measure unit, 1 Sheng equals 4 kilograms.

②　Dou：a monetary and measure unit. 1 Dou equals 10 Sheng.

③　Qian：a monetary and measure unit, 1 Qian equals five grams.

④　Tael：a monetary and measure unit, 1 Tael equals 10 Qian.

女：小哥用真心来赎小妹，
小哥用金银来赎小妹，
婆家答应了，
爹妈也答应了。

男：小妹啊！
小哥讨小妹，
小妹嫁小哥，
从此我们成一家。
鱼儿跟水走，
水顺笕槽流，
竹鸡跟着野鸡走，
小妹快跟小哥走。

女：家里有爹妈，
小妹舍不得。

男：送你爹爹三升马蹄金，
送你妈妈三升驴蹄银。

女：家里亲哥亲兄弟，
小妹舍不得。

男：送你阿哥三把刀，
送你阿弟三把锄。

女：家里阿姐和阿妹，
小妹舍不得。

Woman: You did show your sincere heart,

You did spend gold and silver to bail me out.

That man's family has agreed,

And my family has agreed.


MAN: Oh! My lady!

I marry you,

You marry me.

We set up a family.

Fish goes along with water,

Water goes along with channel,

Bamboo chicken goes along with wild chicken,

My lady goes along with me.


WOMAN: I feel reluctant to leave,

Since I will miss my parents.


MAN: I give your father three Sheng of gold as a gift,

I send your mother three Sheng of silver as a gift.


WOMAN: I feel reluctant to leave,

Since I will miss my brothers.


MAN: I send your brother three knives as a gift,

I send your brother three hoes as a gift.


WOMAN: I feel reluctant to leave,

Since I will miss my sisters.

男：送你阿姐三对银耳环，
送你阿妹三副银镯头。

女：还有亲戚和朋友，
小妹舍不得。

男：杀猪宰羊请他们，
煮肉打酒请他们。

女：还有家禽和家畜，
小妹舍不得。
家里红公鸡，
小妹舍不得。
家里大白鹅，
小妹舍不得。
家里老灰鸭，
小妹舍不得。
家里水牛和黄牛，
小妹舍不得。
家里山羊和绵羊，
小妹舍不得。
家里大肥猪，
小妹舍不得。
家里大黄狗，
小妹舍不得。
家里小花猫，
小妹舍不得。
小妹若要走，
猪鸡牛羊也要跟着走。

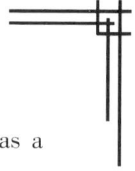

MAN: I send your sisters three pairs of silver earrings as a
gift,

I send your sisters three pairs of silver bracelets as a gift,

WOMAN: I feel reluctant to leave,

Since I will miss my relatives and friends.

MAN: I entertain them with pork and lamb,

I serve them with meat and wine.

WOMAN: I feel reluctant to leave,

Since I will miss my poultry and livestock.

The red rooster,

I will miss it.

The white goose,

I will miss it.

The gray duck,

I will miss it.

The buffalo and cow,

I will miss them.

The fat pig,

I will miss it.

The yellow dog,

I will miss it.

The little cat,

I will miss it.

If I leave,

They will follow me.

男：小哥想办法，
把猪鸡牛羊哄在家。
喂鸡三升谷，
喂鹅三升豆，
喂鸭三升米，
喂牛三把草，
喂羊三枝叶，
喂猪三升糠，
喂狗三个骨头，
糯米饭舀三碗，
喂给小花猫。

女：家里正房后房各三间，
小妹舍不得。

男：正房里烧下三堆火，
后房里堆下三把草。

女：家里粮仓和水槽，
小妹舍不得。

男：粮仓头装下三斗粮，
水槽里挑下三挑水。

女：家里箱子和柜子，
小妹舍不得。

男：箱子里装下三丈布，
柜子头装下三件衣。

MAN: I come up with a solution,
To keep your poultry and livestock at home,
I feed the chickens three Sheng of grain,
I feed geese three Sheng of beans,
I feed ducks three Sheng of rice,
I feed cows three bunches of grass,
I feed sheep three bunches of leaves,
I feed pigs three Sheng of bran,
I feed dogs three bones,
I feed cats
Three bowls of sticky rice.

WOMAN: I feel reluctant to leave,
Since I will miss these six rooms in my house.

MAN: I warm the rooms with three fires,
I leave three stacks of grass in the backroom for future use.

WOMAN: I feel reluctant to leave,
Since I will miss the granary and sink.

MAN: I leave three Dou of grain in the granary,
I leave three Dou of water in the sink.

WOMAN: I feel reluctant to leave,
Since I will miss the chests and cabinets.

MAN: I leave three Zhang of cloth in the chests,
I leave three items of clothing in the cabinets.

女：家里装碗筷的篮子，
小妹舍不得。

男：篮子头装下白碗三个，
篮子头装下筷子三双。
样样安排好，
小妹走得了。

女：小哥啊！
小妹头上无新帽，
身上无新衣，
脚上无新鞋，
穿的破烂出不来，
戴的破烂出不来。

男：小妹啊！
穿的不好不要怕，
戴的不好不要愁，
小哥想办法，
街头有花帽，
街中有花布，
街尾有花鞋。
马蹄金子我背着，
驴蹄银子我背着，
哥妹欢欢喜喜去赶街。
街头买花帽，
街中买花布，
街尾买花鞋。
小妹头上戴花帽，

WOMAN: I feel reluctant to leave,

Since I will miss the utensil caddy.


MAN: I leave three white bowls,

I leave three pairs of chopsticks in the caddy,

I have everything well arranged,

You will come with me with no worry.


WOMAN: Oh! My man!

I do not have a new hat,

I do not have any new clothes,

I do not have any new shoes,

I will not go with you in shabby clothes,

I will not go with you in old shoes,


MAN: Oh! My lady!

Do not worry about your shabby clothes,

Do not worry about your old things,

I have solutions.

There are beautiful hats sold on one end of the street,

There is colorful cloth sold in the middle of the street,

There are pretty shoes sold on the other end of the street,

I take you to buy new things

With gold and silver in hand,

We go shopping together happily.

We buy beautiful hats on one end of the street,

We buy colorful cloth in the middle of the street,

We buy pretty shoes on the other end of the street,

手上戴银镯，
身上披花衣，
脚上穿花鞋。
浑身上下银花开，
从头到脚打扮好，
小妹走得了。

女：小哥啊！
小妹没有好花戴，
没有花戴出不来。

男：小妹啊！
没有花戴不要怕，
小哥上山坡，
采来二月红山茶，
茶花头上戴，
茶花腰上挂，
茶花脚上插。
小妹从头红到脚
小妹从头亮到脚，
这回走得了。

女：有心跟哥走，
就是路没有。

男：大理生铁好，
打把好条锄，
打把好腰斧，

You wear beautiful hats,
You put on silver bracelets,
You wear colorful shoes,
From head to toe,
You are so beautiful.
Now you will go with me.

WOMAN: Oh! My man!
I am not ready to leave,
With no flowers to wear.

MAN: Oh! My lady!
Do not worry about flowers,
I climb up the mountains,
To pick tea flowers of February,
You put them on your head,
You put them on your belt,
You put them on your shoes.
From head to toe,
You are so beautiful.
Now you will come with me.

WOMAN: I'm willing to go with you,
Yet there is no path to walk on.

MAN: The cast iron from Dali is good,
I get some to make a good hoe,
I get some to make a good axe,

打把好钩刀，
小哥来开路。

女：小哥来开路，
越挖路越长，
越挖路越窄。
路长路窄难走过，
只有乌鸦喜鹊才能走，
小妹不能走。

男：小妹不能走，
小哥从头挖。
挖路到松林，
松树哪个砍？

女：挖路到松林，
请啄木鸟来啄。

男：挖路到石岩，
石岩哪个挖？

女：挖路到石岩，
请古字子①来挖。

男：路也挖通了，
小妹快快走。

————————

① 古字子：鸟名。

I get some to make a good knife,

Then I open up a path for you.


WOMAN: My dear man opens up a path,

The path gets longer and longer,

And the path gets narrower and narrower.

The long and narrow path is difficult to take,

It is good for crows and magpies,

But not for me.


MAN: This path does not work for you,

I start over and open up another new one.

This new path goes through pine woods,

And who will help me to cut the pine trees?


WOMAN: Your new path goes through pine woods,

You can ask woodpeckers to help.


MAN: This new path goes through rocks,

And who will help me to excavate the rocks?


WOMAN: The new path goes through rocks,

You can ask Guzizi① bird to help.


MAN: This new path is now finished,

You will come with me now.

---

① Guzizi, name of a bird.

女：小妹出嫁有了路，
老牛前面走，
哥妹跟后头，
来到十一条河，
来到十二条河，
忽见洪水涨，
波浪滚滚来，
小妹不敢过河去。

男：小妹不要怕，
小哥上山砍棵树，
搭上一座桥，
扶妹过桥去。

女：路上有老虎，
路下有豹子，
路心头有大麻蛇。
小妹最怕老虎，
小妹最怕豹子，
小妹最怕大麻蛇。

男：人说小米小，
小妹的胆子比小米小。
路上不是虎，
是个大石头。
路下不是豹，
是个老树根。
路心不是大麻蛇，
放羊娃娃掉下一根赶羊鞭。

WOMAN: Now I have a path to take,

The old ox leads the way,

We follow the ox,

We come to the Eleven river,

We come to the Twelve river,

Flood is coming suddenly,

Waves are rushing rapidly,

I'm too scared to cross the river.


MAN: My lady, do not be scared,

I cut a tree down on the mountains,

And I build a bridge,

I hold you tight while we go across the bridge.


WOMAN: There is a tiger in our way,

There is a leopard in our way,

There is a big spotted snake in our way.

I'm afraid of tigers the most,

I'm afraid of leopards the most,

I'm afraid of snakes the most.


MAN: It is said that millet is small,

Yet your courage is smaller than that.

There is no tiger in the way,

It is actually a rock.

There is no leopard in the way,

It is actually a tree stump.

There is no snake in the way,

It is actually a sheep whip lost by a shepherd.

女：路边青草上，
为何有油水？
小妹心害怕。

男：不是草上有油水，
露水落在青草上，
太阳出来晒一晒，
露水就干了。

女：一面走来一面听，
路上路下有声音，
小妹不敢走。

男：小妹不要怕，
路上有声音，
是小貂鼠在跑；
路下有声音，
是小雀飞起来。

女：小哥啊！
怎么树上挂篮子？
怎么路心头垫虎皮？
小妹没见过。

男：树上没有挂篮子，
那是小雀窝；

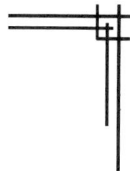

WOMAN: Why is there grease
On the grass on the way?
I do not overcome my fear.

MAN: It is dew on the grass,
It is not grease.
When exposed in the sun
It will soon dry out.

WOMAN: I hear some noise,
While I take my steps.
I'm scared to go forward.

MAN: My lady, do not be scared,
A little mouse is running,
That is why there is some noise from below;
A little bird is flying away,
That is why there is some noise from above.

WOMAN: Oh! My man!
Why is there a basket hanging on the tree?
Why is there a tiger's skin laying on the road?
I have not seen these before.

MAN: There is no basket on the tree,
It is a bird's nest.

路心没有垫虎皮，
那是树影子。
小妹胆莫小，
只管放心走。

女：走到小哥家门前，
小妹抬头看一看，
有些飞鸟来卖针，
小妹胆子小，
不敢进门槛。

男：小妹不要怕，
飞的不是鸟，
我家蜜蜂采花回，
不是鸟卖针，
蜜蜂身上有蜂刺。

女：来到小哥家，
小哥家里老虎叫，
小哥家里豹子吼，
小妹很害怕。

男：小妹不要怕，
不是老虎叫，
不是豹子吼；
亲戚朋友接小妹，
吹着唢呐接小妹，
敲锣打鼓接小妹。

There is no tiger's skin on the road,

It is a shadow of a tree.

My lady, do not be scared,

You will go ahead.


WOMAN: When I arrive at your house,

I look up and find some birds,

They are carrying needles.

I'm too afraid

And dare not to go inside.


MAN: My lady, do not be afraid,

The flying creatures are not birds,

But the domestic bees I raise,

Those are not needles carried by birds,

But stings of bees.


WOMAN: When I arrive at your house,

I hear tigers roaring inside,

I hear leopards howling inside,

I'm really scared.


MAN: My lady, do not be scared,

There are no roaring tigers,

There are no howling leopards;

The sounds are from my relatives and friends,

They are playing Suona to welcome you,

They are playing drums and gongs to welcome you.

女：妹跟小哥进了门，
院头开银花，
院中栽虎骨，
院尾开金花。

男：院头不是开银花，
要办喜事搭彩棚；
院中不是栽虎骨，
搭棚用的松树桩；
院尾不是开金花，
院尾搭起锥栗架。

女：进了哥家门，
小妹无房住。

男：小妹无房住，
小哥挖地基。

女：地基挖好了，
哪个量地基？
哪个看地基？
哪个滚地基？

男：公鸡量地基，
公鸡看地基，
公鸡滚地基。

女：地基量好了，
怎么盖房子？

WOMAN: I step into your house after you,
There are silver flowers in the front yard,
There are tiger bones sticking in the central yard,
There are gold flowers in the back yard.

MAN: There is no silver flower in the front yard,
but a decorated tent for the wedding ceremony.
There are no tiger bones sticking in the central yard,
But pine stumps for building a tent;
There is no gold flower in the back yard,
But a chestnut pergola.

WOMAN: I come into your house,
But find no room for me to live.

MAN: My lady has no room to live,
I dig a foundation and build one for you.

WOMAN: The foundation is ready,
Who measure it?
Who inspect it?
Who check it?

MAN: The rooster measures it,
The rooster inspects it,
The rooster checks it.

WOMAN: The foundation is set,
How do you build a house on it?

男：哥妹来商量：
小哥翘起拇指好算年，
小妹掐着食指好算月。
到了正二月，
上山砍木料，
松头做椽子，
松杆做过梁，
松根做柱子。
到了三四月，
木头晒干了，
小哥上山抬木头。

女：木头抬回来，
哪个钻木头？

男：木头抬回来，
请啄木鸟钻木头。

女：用什么量木头？
用什么弹墨线？

男：尺子量木头，
墨斗弹墨线。

女：哪个合木头？
哪个竖过梁？

MAN：You and I make a plan together.

I select a good year,

You select a good month.

When the February comes,

I go up the hills for logging.

I take pine treetops to build rafters,

I take pine trunks to build roof beam,

I take pine roots to build pillars.

When the March and April come,

Timbers are completely dried,

I go up the hills and haul them back.

WOMAN：You haul timbers back,

Who drill them?

MAN：I ask woodpeckers to help,

Woodpeckers drill the timbers.

WOMAN：What do you use to measure the timbers?

What do you use to mark the line?

MAN：I take a ruler to measure the timbers,

I take an ink marker to mark the line.

WOMAN：Who fits these timbers together?

Who erects roof beams?

男：木匠合木头，
　木匠竖过梁。

女：木头合好了，
　过梁竖好了，
　哪个盖房子？

男：房架竖好了，
　木匠来盖房。

女：割草盖草房，
　烧瓦盖瓦房，
　小妹进了房，
　房里没有床。

男：松板来做床，
　竹席做垫子。

女：飞蚊做了窝，
　鸳鸯鸟成双，
　我们两个安家了。

男：哥妹去赶街，
　二十二两白银买水牛，
　二十二两白银买驮马；
　买了绵羊买山羊，
　样样买齐全。

356

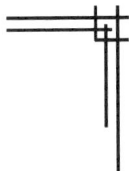

MAN: The carpenter fits these timbers together,
The carpenter erects roof beams.

WOMAN: The timbers are fitted together,
The roof beams are well erected,
Who builds the house?

MAN: The framework was well erected,
The carpenter builds the house.

WOMAN: We reap hay to make a hay house,
We make tiles to make a tile-roofed house,
After entering the house,
I find there is no bed.

MAN: I take a pine board as a bed,
I take a bamboo mat as a mattress.

WOMAN: Mosquitos make nests,
Mandarin ducks get matched,
You and I settle down.

MAN: We go to the shopping street,
And buy buffalos with twenty-two taels of silver,
And buy horses with twenty-two taels of silver.
We buy sheep and goats,
We buy all that we need.

女：鸡猪牛羊关满圈，
我们两个啊，
养的牛多起来了，
养的羊多起来了！

男：小妹在家放牛羊，
小哥上街买种子。
走到街上看粮食，
粮仓十二间，
一间装谷子，
一间装荞子，
一间装包谷，
一间装麻子，
一间装麦子，
一间装豆子，
样样都齐全。
好的种子给三文，
坏的种子给两文。
谷子买三箩，
荞子买三箩，
包谷买三箩，
麻子买三箩，
麦子买三箩，
豆子买三箩，
样样种子买齐全。

女：小哥小妹开了田地，
小哥小妹找到放牛羊的地方，

WOMAN: We keep livestock in the yard,

You and I,

We raise more and more cattle,

We raise more and more sheep.


MAN: My lady herd cattle and sheep back at home,

I go to town to buy seeds,

I find grain seeds sold in the shopping street,

There are twelve granaries,

One for storing millet,

One for storing buckwheat,

One for storing corn,

One for storing flax seeds,

One for storing wheat,

One for storing beans,

Here is everything that we need.

I pay three coins for seeds of good quality,

I pay two coins for seeds of poor quality,

I buy three baskets of millet,

I buy three baskets of buckwheat,

I buy three baskets of corn,

I buy three baskets of flax seeds,

I buy three baskets of wheat,

I buy three baskets of beans,

I buy everything that we need.


WOMAN: We pick a good place to plow,

We pick a good place to herd,

照着年月节令耪庄稼,
照着年月节令放牛羊。

男：正月初二到,
动手撒秧了,
犁头犁架动起来,
先耪河边有水田。

女：小妹筛出种子来,
小妹簸出种子来,
小哥背去河里泡。

男：正月初二撒小秧,
二月初二秧出土
三月初二秧长大。
到了五月间,
栽秧季节到,
头棵秧苗哥来栽,
秧苗长得绿莹莹,
草也长得秧样高,
小妹你快薅秧去。

女：小妹力气小,
抓不起稗子拔不起草。
薅秧薅到五月间,
紧薅薅不完。
小哥啊!
你不是撒秧是撒草。

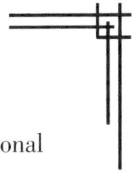

We grow grain in accordance with the laws of seasonal arrangements,

We herd in accordance with the laws of seasonal arrangements.

MAN: When January second comes,

I start to sow seeds,

Plows start to work,

I begin with the paddy fields by the river.

WOMAN: I sieve seeds out,

I select seeds out,

You take them to soak in the river.

MAN: Seeds are sowed on January second,

Seedlings sprout on February second,

Seedlings grow on March second.

May comes,

The sowing season arrives,

I plant seedlings for the first round.

Seedlings grow well and fast,

Weeds grow as well,

My lady, you need to weed them out.

WOMAN: I do not have enough strength,

And I can not pull up tares and weeds.

I have been weeding since mid-May,

But I can not get it all done.

Oh! My man!

You sow more weed seeds than grain.

男：小妹啊！
抓不动的草有十二种，
抓得动的草有十二种；
拔不动的草有十二种，
拔得动的草有十二种；
硬的草有十二种，
软的草有十二种。
小哥力气大，
抓不动的草哥去抓，
拔不动的草哥去拔。
小妹力气小，
抓得动的草妹去抓，
拔得动的草妹去拔。
杂草稗子小哥分不清，
要请小妹教小哥。

女：小哥听妹说：
抓不动的是牙齿草，
拔不动的是稗子。

男：正月接二月，
正合撒麻子，
麻子出得绿油油；
三月接四月，
正合撒荞子，
荞子出得绿又嫩；

MAN: Oh! My lady!

There are twelve kinds of weeds that are hard to pull,

There are twelve kinds of weeds that are easy to pull,

There are twelve kinds of weeds that are hard to uproot,

There are twelve kinds of weeds that are easy to uproot.

There are twelve kinds of hard weeds,

There are twelve kinds of soft weeds.

I have enough strength,

I will pull hard weeds,

I will uproot hard weeds.

You do not have much strength,

You will pull soft weeds,

You will uproot soft weeds.

But I can not tell tares and weeds apart,

Please teach me how to distinguish between them.


WOMAN: Well, you listen to me,

Yachi grass① is difficult to pull out,

Tare is hard to uproot.


MAN: January and February,

It is the right season to sow flax seeds,

Flax grows well and fast.

March and April,

It is the right season to sow buckwheat seeds,

Buckwheat grows well and fast.

---

① Yachi grass: one kind of weed, the shape of which is like teeth.

六月屋后撒萝卜，
萝卜长得粗又长；
七月割甜荞，
甜荞装满袋，
七月十四尝新荞；
八月谷子低着头，
谷穗像马尾，
拿起镰刀下田去，
割谷晒谷忙。
谷子背回家，
属蛇日来尝。

女：哪个来割麻？
哪个来刷麻？

男：小妹来割麻，
小哥来刷麻。
小妹拿起镰刀来割麻，
小哥拿起梨树板子来刷麻。

女：哪个抱麻秸？
哪个掰麻枝？

男：小哥抱麻秸，
小妹掰麻枝。

女：麻皮哪里晒？
麻皮哪里泡？

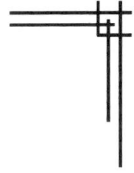

Carrot seeds are sowed in back yard in June,

Carrots grow long and thick.

Buckwheat is reaped in July,

The harvest fills a full package,

On July fourteenth we try them for food.

Millet is mature in August,

Ears of millet look like pony tails.

I go to the fields with a sickle,

And I am busy reaping and drying grain.

I carry grain back home,

And try them for food on a day of the snake.


WOMAN: Who reaps flax?

Who peels flax?


MAN: You reap flax,

I peel flax.

You reap flax with a sickle,

I peel flax with a piece of pear wood.


WOMAN: Who takes flax stems away?

Who breaks flax stems open?


MAN: I take flax stems away,

You break flax stems open.


WOMAN: Where do we dry flax skins?

Where do we soak flax skins?

男：松树杆上晒，
河水深处泡。

女：麻皮哪里洗？

男：河里青石板上洗。
哪个来绩麻？

女：小妹来绩麻。
二指把麻绕，
大指把麻分。

男：哪个来纺线？

女：小妹来纺线。
大锅来煮线，
煮线煮出来，
青石板上洗，
房前屋后晒。

男：哪个来织布？

女：小妹来织布。
麻布织出来，
拿去街上换，
麻布换细布，
两丈换一丈。
麻布换花布，

MAN: We dry them on pine trunks,

We soak them deep in the river.

WOMAN: Where do we wash them?

MAN: We wash them on surface of river stones.

Who twists flax into threads?

WOMAN: I twist flax into threads,

I bind them with my index finger,

I divide them with my thumb.

MAN: Who spins threads?

WOMAN: I spin threads.

I boil thread in a big pot,

The thread is boiled

And then washed on surface of flat stones,

And dried in front yard and back yard of the house.

MAN: Who weaves threads into cloth?

WOMAN: I weave threads into cloth.

When flax cloth is made,

I trade it in the shopping street,

I trade two Zhang of flax cloth,

For one Zhang of fine cotton cloth.

I trade three Zhang of flax cloth,

三丈换一丈。
青布白布夹杂缝，
花衣装满箱。

男：楼上谷子堆满仓，
楼下荞子装满囤，
养牛牛满圈，
养羊羊满圈，
养马马满圈，
养猪猪满圈，
养鸡鸡满圈。

小妹啊！
日子过得好，
日子过得长。
生了好儿子，
生了好姑娘。
儿子长大放牛羊，
姑娘长大织布缝衣裳。

For one Zhang of pattern-designed cloth.

Trunks are filled with colorful clothes,

As well as blue and white cloth.


MAN: We have grain filling the granary upstairs,

We have buckwheat filling the granary downstairs,

We have cattle filling in the pen,

We have sheep filling in the yard,

We have horses filling in the stable,

We have pigs filling in the sty,

We have chickens filling in the henhouse,


Oh! My lady!

We have a good life,

We will live a long life.

We will have healthy sons,

We will have healthy daughters.

Our sons will herd cows and sheep when they grow up,

Our daughters will weave cloth and make clothes when they

grow up.

# 第四部 丧 葬

## 一、死亡

天王撒下活种子，
天王撒下死种子。
活的种子筛一角，
死的种子筛三筛。
活的种子撒一把，
死的种子撒三把。

死种撒出去，
会让的就能活在世上，
不会让的就死亡。

六月七月间，
死种撒到白云上，
死种撒到黑云上，
白云黑云都会让。

八月九月间，
死种撒到月亮上，
月亮也会让。

# Chapter Four    Funeral

## Section One    Death

Lord Gezi scatters seeds of life,
Lord Gezi scatters seeds of death.
He throws one handful of seeds of life,
And three handfuls of seeds of death.
He casts one handful of seeds of life,
And three handfuls of seeds of death.

When seeds of death are scattered,
Those who know how to avoid them will live,
Those who do not, will die.

In June and July,
Seeds of death are scattered on white clouds,
Seeds of death are scattered on black clouds,
White and black clouds both know how to stay away from them.

In August and September,
Seeds of death are scattered on the moon,
The moon knows how to stay away from them.

十冬腊月天，
死种撒到星星上，
星星也会让。

正二三月春天来，
死种撒到节令上，
节令也会让。
死种撒地上，
大地不会让，
地会裂成缝。
死种撒到山头上，
山也不会让，
山会塌下来
死种撒到石岩上，
石岩不会让，
石岩会裂开。
死种撒到树头上，
树也不会让，
树子会死亡；
撒到橡子树头上，
橡子树就死了；
撒到柏枝树头上，
柏枝树就死了；
撒到赤松树头上，
赤松树也死了；
撒到梧桐树头上，

In October, November and December,

Seeds of death are scattered on the stars,

The stars know how to stay away from them.

When spring is here in January, February and March,

Seeds of death are scattered on the seasons,

Seasons know how to stay away from them.

Seeds of death are scattered on the ground,

The earth does not know how to stay away from them,

And thus the earth cracks.

Seeds of death are scattered on top of mountains,

Mountains do not know how to stay away from them,

And thus mountains collapse.

Seeds of death are scattered on rocks,

Rocks do not know how to stay away from them,

And thus rocks crack up.

Seeds of death are scattered on trees,

Trees do not know how to stay away from them,

And thus trees die.

Seeds of death are scattered on oak trees,

And thus oak trees die.

Seeds of death are scattered on cypress trees,

And thus cypress trees die.

Seeds of death are scattered on red pines,

And thus red pine trees die.

Seeds of death are scattered on phoenix trees,

梧桐树也死了。
撒到杨柳树头上，
杨柳树也死了；
撒到马缨花树上，
马缨花树不开花；
撒到橄榄树头上，
橄榄树也死了；
撒到花椒树头上，
花椒树也死了；
撒到竹子上，
竹子会枯死。

地上树木都撒遍，
地上树木都会死。
没有撒不到的树，
没有不会死的树。

死种撒到草头上，
草不会让，
草会死亡。
撒在地面草尖上，
地上的草会枯黄。

撒到芦苇上，
芦苇会枯死；
撒到山草上，
山草就会死；
撒到艾草上，

And thus phoenix trees die.

Seeds of death are scattered on willow trees,

And thus willow trees die.

Seeds of death are scattered on Mayinghua trees,

And thus Mayinghua trees do not blossom.

Seeds of death are scattered on olive trees,

And thus olive trees die.

Seeds of death are scattered on pepper trees,

And thus pepper trees die.

Seeds of death are scattered on bamboo,

And thus bamboo dies.


All trees are scattered with seeds of death,

And thus all trees will die.

There is no exception,

No tree is immortal.


Seeds of death are scattered on grass,

Grass will not be able to stay away from them,

And thus grass will die.

Seeds of death are scattered on grass,

And thus grass will turn yellow and wither.


Seeds of death are scattered on reeds,

And thus reeds will die.

Seeds of death are scattered on mountain grass,

And thus mountain grass will die.

Seeds of death are scattered on wormwoods,

艾草会枯死；
撒到黄麻上，
黄麻就会死。

地上的草都撒遍，
地上的草都会死。
没有撒不到的草，
没有不会死的草。

死种撒到百兽头顶上，
百兽不会让，
百兽会死亡。

撒到兔子头顶上，
兔子会被石头打死；
撒到老虎头顶上，
老虎会钻在猎人的木圈里；
撒到野猪头顶上，
野猪会被猎人打死；
撒到獐子麂子头顶上，
獐子麂子会跑进猎人的网里；
撒到狐狸头顶上，
狐狸会跑进猎人网里；
撒到大熊小熊头顶上，
大熊小熊会跳进陷阱里。

百兽都撒遍了，
百兽都会死。

And thus wormwoods will die.

Seeds of death are scattered on jutes,

And thus jutes will die.


All grass is scattered with seeds of death,

And thus all grass will die eventually.

There is no exception,

No grass is immortal.


Seeds of death are scattered on animals,

Animals will not be able to stay away from them,

And thus all animals will die.


Seeds of death are scattered on rabbits,

And rabbits will be hit and killed by stones.

Seeds of death are scattered on tigers,

And tigers will be trapped by hunters.

Seeds of death are scattered on boars,

And boars will be killed by hunters.

Seeds of death are scattered on river deer and muntjacs,

And river deer and muntjacs will run into hunters' traps.

Seeds of death are scattered on foxes,

And foxes will fall into hunters' nets.

Seeds of death are scattered on big and small bears,

And big and small bears will step into hunters' traps.


All animals are scattered with seeds of death,

And thus all animals will die eventually.

没有撒不到的兽，
没有不会死的兽。

死种撒到百鸟头顶上，
百鸟不会让，
百鸟会死亡。

撒到凤凰头顶上，
凤凰飞进网里死；
撒到大雁头顶上，
大雁在高山顶上死；
撒到野鸡头顶上，
野鸡踩着扣子死；
撒到啄木鸟头顶上，
啄木鸟折断脖子死；
撒到画眉头顶上，
画眉也会死；
撒到杂雀头顶上，
杂雀都会死。

百鸟都撒遍了，
百鸟都会死。
就连春天布谷鸟，
就连河中洗衣鸟，
也都撒到了。
没有撒不到的鸟，
没有不会死的鸟。
死种撒到百虫头顶上，

There is no exception,

No animal is immortal.


Seeds of death are scattered on birds,

And birds do not know how to stay away from them,

And thus all birds will die.


Seeds of death are scattered on phoenixes,

And phoenixes will get into hunters' snares.

Seeds of death are scattered on wild geese,

And wild geese will die on the top of mountains.

Seeds of death are scattered on pheasants,

And pheasants will be caught by hunters' traps.

Seeds of death are scattered on woodpeckers,

And woodpeckers will break their necks.

Seeds of death are scattered on thrushes,

And thrushes will die.

Seeds of death are scattered on other birds,

And other birds will die.


All birds are scattered with seeds of death,

And thus all birds will die.

Even cuckoos in spring,

Even birds in rivers,

They are also scattered with seeds of death.

There is no exception,

No bird is immortal.

Seeds of death are scattered on all insects,

百虫不会让，
百虫会死亡。

撒到大马蜂头顶上，
大马蜂在风雪中冻死；
撒到蚂蚱头顶上，
蚂蚱会被火烧死；
撒到苍蝇蚊子头顶上，
苍蝇蚊子会被药毒死；
撒到蚯蚓头顶上，
蚯蚓会被锄头挖死。

百虫都撒遍了，
百虫都会死。
没有撒不到的虫，
没有不会死的虫。

死种撒到鱼儿头顶上，
鱼儿不会让，
鱼儿会死亡。

撒到鱼儿头顶上，
鱼儿跳进鱼网死；
撒到石蚌头顶上，
石蚌也会跳进网里死。

鱼儿都撒遍了，
鱼儿都会死。

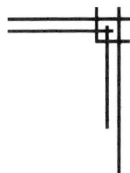

All insects do not know how to stay away from them,
And thus insects will die.

Seeds of death are scattered on wasps,
And wasps will be frozen to death in snow storms.
Seeds of death are scattered on grasshoppers,
And grasshoppers will be burned in fire.
Seeds of death are scattered on flies and mosquitos,
And flies and mosquitos will be poisoned by drugs.
Seeds of death are scattered on earthworms,
And earthworms will be hit by hoes.

All insects are scattered with seeds of death,
And thus all insects will die.
There is no exception,
No insect is immortal.

Seeds of death are scattered on fish,
Fish do not know how to stay away from them,
And thus fish will die.

Seeds of death are scattered on fish,
And fish will bump into fishing nets.
Seeds of death are scattered on clams,
And clams will jump into fishing nets.

All fish are scattered with seeds of death,
And thus all fish will die.

没有撒不到的鱼，
没有不会死的鱼。

死种撒在家畜头顶上，
家畜不会让，
家畜会死亡。

撒到黄牛头顶上，
黄牛犁地会累死；
撒到肥猪头顶上，
肥猪过年要杀死；
撒到绵羊头顶上，
绵羊在山上跌死。

家畜都撒遍了，
家畜都会死。
没有撒不到的家畜，
没有不会死的家畜。

四月撒死种，
八月会死完。
鸟兽鱼虫都撒遍，
鸟兽鱼虫都会死。
撒也撒完了，
死也死完了。
没有撒不到的东西，
没有不会死的东西。

There is no exception,

No fish is immortal.


Seeds of death are scattered on livestock,

And livestock do not know how to stay away from them,

And thus livestock will die.


Seeds of death are scattered on cattle,

And cattle will be worn out to death.

Seeds of death are scattered on fat pigs,

And fat pigs will be sacrificed on Spring Festival.

Seeds of death are scattered on sheep,

And sheep will fall off mountains.


All livestock are scattered with seeds of death,

And thus all livestock will die.

There is no exception,

No livestock is immortal.


If seeds of death are scattered in April,

All creatures will die out by August.

If all animals and insects are scattered with seeds of death,

All animals and insects will die out.

If all seeds of death are scattered,

All creatures will die out.

There is no exception,

Nothing is immortal.

早晨太阳出，
晚上太阳落，
太阳会出也会落。
人和太阳一个样，
会生也会死。

高山长树木，
发出嫩芽绿又旺，
长出叶来也很稳。
只说高山树木不落叶，
哪知九月叶会黄，
风吹黄叶叶就落。
人死就像落叶样，
到死时候也会死。

灶洞烧火要有风，
没风烧火火褪色，
没风烧火火会灭；
人死就像火褪色，
人死就像火会灭，
到死时候也会死。

田头梨子树，
二月开花长出叶，
三月四月会结果，
五月六月果子稳，
七月八月果子熟，
籽饱果熟就掉下，

The sun goes up in the mornings,

The sun goes down in the evenings,

The sun always goes up and down.

People are the same.

People are born and people die.


Trees grow on high mountains,

They start with green and lush buds,

And grow into strong and firm leaves.

It is believed that those tree leaves would never fall,

But these leaves would turn yellow in September.

Yellow leaves fall while wind blowing.

People die like leaves fall,

People will die when it is time.


People need wind to set fire in the oven,

Fire will fade away without wind,

Fire will extinguish without wind.

People die like fire fades,

People die like fire extinguishes,

People will die when it is time.


Pear trees grow in fields,

They grow leaves and blossom in February,

They bear fruits in March and April,

Their fruits grow larger in May and June,

Their fruits grow mature in July and August,

Fruits fall when they are mature,

人死就像果子掉，
到死时候也会死。

世人都会死，
一百岁的人会死，
三十多岁的人也会死，
几岁的人也会死，
生下地的娃娃也会死；
男人会死，
女人会死；
做大官的人会死，
做小吏的人也会死；
穷人会死，
发财的人也会死。

死种撒下来，
撒到病人头顶上，
病人不会让，
就会病死掉。

阿爹生了病，
要找不死药：
找到昆明去，
找到禄丰去，
找到大理去，
找到白井去，

People die like fruits fall,

People will die when it is time.


No people are immortal,

One-hundred-year-old man can die,

Thirty-year-old man can die,

Three-year-old boy can die,

Babies who are just born can die.

Men can die,

Women can die,

Officials in high position can die,

Petty officials can die.

Poor people can die,

Rich people can die.


When seeds of death are scattered

On sick people,

Sick people do not know how to stay away from them,

And thus they will die from diseases.


My father got sick,

I wanted to find medicines of immortality.

I went to Kunming,

I went to Lufeng①,

I went to Dali,

I went to Baijing,

---

又到姚安找，
又到牟定找，
找过了许多地方。
医疼的药倒有，
医死的药没有。

没有办法了！
只好背爹去躲病。
背到哪里躲？
背到大山上，
松树根边躲。
只说松树万古不会死，
哪知松树也会死！
松树咋个死？
打柴人来劈明子，
劈开松树当火把；
松树被劈死，
还是躲不脱。

山上躲不脱，
背去大箐里，
锥栗树根边躲，
哪知锥栗树也会死！
锥栗树咋个死？
雨水糟树心，
风刮腰断死，
还是躲不脱。

I went to Yao'an,

I went to Mouding,

I went to many regions.

I found that there were only medicines for illness,

But there were no medicines of immortality.


I had no choice,

But to carry my father on my back and try to hide from

diseases.

Where would we go?

We went to a big mountain,

And hid beside a pine.

We thought that pines would not die in millions of years,

But pines would also die.

How could pine trees die?

Pines could be cut down as firewood,

They could be turned into torches.

This pine was cut into pieces,

We could not hide beside the pine tree anymore.


There was nowhere to hide in the mountains anymore,

We went into valleys,

And hid beside a chestnut tree.

Yet, a chestnut tree could also die.

How could a chestnut tree die?

Its roots could be spoiled by water,

Its trunk could be torn down by wind,

We could not hide beside the chestnut tree anymore.

大箐躲不脱，
背去山岩边，
石岩底下躲。
只说石岩下雨不会死，
日晒不会炸，
哪知石岩也会死！
石岩咋个死？
石岩崩裂死，
还是躲不脱。

石岩躲不脱，
背回家里去，
柜子里头躲。
只说柜子里头不进风，
日晒不着，
雨打不着，
哪知柜子也会死！
柜子咋个死？
蛀虫来蛀死，
还是躲不脱。
吃药吃不好，
躲病躲不好，
阿爹死掉了！

高山石头最稳当，
七月下雨也会垮，
石头垮了滚下箐，
滚到箐底不回头。

There was nowhere to hide in the valleys anymore,

We went to boulders,

And hid beside a boulder.

It is said boulders would not die in rainy days,

And boulders would not be parched in sunny days,

But boulders could also die!

How could boulders die?

Boulders could crack and die.

We could not hide beside the boulder anymore.


We could not hide beside boulders anymore,

We went back home,

And hid in a cabinet.

It is said that wind could not blow into the cabinet,

And sunshine could not reach the cabinet,

And rain could not touch the cabinet.

But cabinets can also die.

How can a cabinet die?

It can be eaten up by woodworms,

We can not hide in the cabinets anymore.

My father was not cured by medicines,

He was not able to recover,

And died eventually!


Rocks on mountains were stable,

But in raining days in July, they could fall.

Rocks could fall into valleys,

Without turning or stopping.

阿爹也像石头滚下箐，

阿爹救不活，

阿爹死掉了！


水在秧田里面很稳当，

坝头泥裂不会垮，

种田人来翻埂子，

只见水浪滚出去，

不见水浪折回来。

阿爹也像水浪滚出去，

阿爹救不活，

阿爹死掉了！

## 二、怀亲

我爹我妈来兴家，

松梢做椽子，

松腰做过梁，

松根做柱子，

房子盖得好，

房子修齐了。

家里有儿子，

村里有嫁出去的姑娘。

有满圈的牛，

有成百匹的马，

成千的公羊，

成百的母羊，

My father fell like a stone into the valleys,

He was not able to recover,

And died eventually!

Water in paddy fields was peaceful,

Mud dam had cracks but would not collapse.

But when farmers came to plow the fields,

Water flew everywhere,

Without turning and stopping.

My father was gone like the water,

He was not able to recover,

And died eventually!

# Section Two　Expressing Condolence
# to Parents

My father and mother built the house.

Heads of pines were taken to make rafters,

Waists of pines were taken to make beams,

Feet of pines were taken to make pillars.

A good house was built,

A house was well built.

They had a son,

They had a married daughter.

They had cattle in the shed,

They had horses in the stable,

They had rams in the pen,

They had ewes in the pen,

满槽的黑猪，
满村的家狗，
满院的鸡。

我爹我妈来管家，
事事有头绪，
样样都顺利。
一年有四季，
一季三个月；
我爹和我妈，
大拇指算年，
小拇指算月，
算着年月耪庄稼。
正月撒小秧，
二月三月到，
山坡上面撒荞子，
山腰上面撒小米；
四月栽秧忙，
山脚河边栽小秧，
包谷撒在房后头，
麦瓜黄瓜房前种。

庄稼长得好，
荞子像葡萄，
小米穗像团白麻线，
谷穗像马尾，
好麻像竹林。
麦瓜和黄瓜，

They had black pigs in the sty,

They had dogs running around in the village,

They had chickens in the yard.


My father and mother managed house affairs.

Everything was arranged properly,

Everything went smoothly.

They worked for four seasons every year,

They worked three months every season.

My father and mother,

They counted years with thumbs,

They counted months with pinky fingers,

They counted time to grow crops.

In January, they planted small seedlings,

In February and March,

They scattered buckwheat seeds on the hill slopes,

They scattered millet seeds on hill sides.

In April, they were busy planting rice.

Rice were planted by the river at the foot of the hills.

Corn seeds were scattered in back of the house,

Cucumbers and pumpkins were planted in front of the house.


Crops all grew very well.

Buckwheat looked like grapes,

Ears of millet looked like balls of flax twine,

Ears of grain looked like ponytails,

Strong flax plants looked like bamboo forests.

Pumpkins and cucumbers were flourishing,

一棵发十棵，
瓜儿结得好，
瓜儿结得多，
庄稼长得好，
粮食堆满仓。

好家不出好事情：
房顶上结了蜘蛛网，
梁上挂着葫芦包，
马鬃被虫咬，
马尾被鼠咬，
公牛的角开了花，
母牛下双儿，
母狗下独儿，
牙狗半夜三更哭，
公鸡叫不出声来，
母鸡下软蛋，
花衣花布装满柜，
尽被虫吃老鼠咬，
缝衣裳啊缝歪了，
麻团中间躲苍蝇。

好麻长得不像竹林，
麻头成了蜘蛛网；
荞子长得不像葡萄，
荞子开花不结子；
小米长得不像白麻线，

With one seedling growing into ten.

Their fruits were large and healthy,

It was a huge harvest.

Crops all grew well and strong,

Barns were filled with harvests.


This happy family encountered bad things:

There were spider webs on the ceiling,

There was a gourd hanging from the beam,

The mane of their horse was bitten by insects,

The tail of their horse was bitten by mice,

The horns of their ox were broken,

Their cow gave birth to twins,

Their dog gave birth to a single puppy

Which cried in the mid-night,

Their rooster lost its voice,

Their hen laid shapeless eggs,

Their cabinet was filled with colorful clothes

Which were all bitten by pests and mice.

Their clothes could not be sewed well,

Because flies were hidden in flax twine balls.


The good flax plants were no longer flourishing like bamboo forest,

Their heads looked like a spider web.

Buckwheat was no longer as big as grapes,

It blossomed but bear no fruit.

Ears of millet were no longer like flax twine balls,

成了白穗子；
谷子长得不像马尾，
变成了鸟窝。
这些不是好事情。

我爹属龙那天病，
我妈属蛇那天病。
河里白鱼尾巴跳，
我爹病倒在床头，
我妈病倒在床尾。
左手拉我爹，
右手扶我妈，
拉也拉不住，
扶也扶不稳。

房前跟弟弟商量，
房后跟哥哥商量，
替爹来送鬼，
替妈来送鬼。
拿红梨枝送鬼，
拿白梨枝送鬼。
把鬼送到松山头，
把鬼送到松山坡。
鬼已送过了，
我爹的病没有好，
我妈的病没有好。

房前跟弟弟商量，
房后跟哥哥商量，

They were bare and empty.

Ears of wheat were no longer like ponytails,

They became birds' nests.

All bad things happened.


My father got sick on a day of the dragon,

My mother got sick on a day of the snake.

There were white fish wagging their tails in rivers.

My father lay in one side of the bed,

My mother lay in the other side of the bed.

I held my father with my left hand,

I held my mother with my right hand,

But I could not hold them well,

And I could not keep balance well.


I talked to my little brother in front of the house,

I talked to my big brother in back of the house,

We would drive the evil spirits away for our father,

We would drive the evil spirits away for our mother.

We drove the evil spirits away with a red pear tree twig,

We drove the evil spirits away with a white pear tree twig.

We sent the evil spirits away to the hilltop,

We sent the evil spirits away to the hill slope.

Although we sent the evil spirits away,

My father did not recover,

My mother did not recover.


I talked to my little brother in front of the house,

I talked to my big brother in back of the house,

替爹来祭神，
替妈来祭神。
祭神没有跳神匠，
祭神要有跳神匠。
左手拿起三炷香，
右手提起三升米，
再拿三块白盐巴，
去找跳神匠。

一找找着泥瓦匠：
"三炷香我不接，
三升白米我不收，
三块盐巴我不拿；
我靠烧瓦罐卖瓦罐吃饭，
不当跳神匠。"

再找找到木匠家：
"三炷香我不接，
三升白米我不收，
三块盐巴我不拿；
我靠做木桶卖木桶吃饭，
不当跳神匠。"

去找养马人：
"三炷香我不接，
三升白米我不收，

We decided to make a sacrifice to gods for our father,

We decided to make a sacrifice to gods for our mother.

We decided to conduct a worship ceremony,

And to invite a sacrificial ritual dancer.

I hold three sticks of incense in my left hand,

I took three Sheng of rice and three chunks of salt in my
right hand,

With all these presents,

I went out to invite a sacrificial ritual dancer.


I found a plasterer first,

But he replied,

"I will not accept your incense,

I will not accept your rice and salt.

I make and sell pots for a living,

I am not a sacrificial ritual dancer."


I found a carpenter later,

But he replied,

"I will not accept your incense,

I will not accept your rice and salt.

I make and sell wooden pots for a living,

I am not a sacrificial ritual dancer."


I found a horse-keeper,

But he replied,

"I will not accept your incense,

三块盐巴我不拿；
我靠养马卖马吃饭，
不当跳神匠。"

去找弓弩匠：
"三炷香我不接，
三升白米我不收，
三块盐巴我不拿；
我靠做弩弓卖弩弓吃饭，
不当跳神匠。"

去找石匠家：
"三炷香我不接，
三升白米我不收，
三块盐巴我不拿；
我靠打石头卖石头吃饭。
不当跳神匠。"

最后找到老朵觋①，
三炷香他接去，
三升白米他收下，
三块盐巴他拿去。
老朵觋说：
"天神我会祭，

---

① 朵觋：即巫师，替人送鬼跳神的人。

I will not accept your rice and salt.

I raise and sell horses for a living,

I am not a sacrificial ritual dancer."


I found a bow-maker,

But he replied,

"I will not accept your incense,

I will not accept your rice and salt.

I make and sell bows for a living,

I am not a sacrificial ritual dancer."


I found a stone-keeper,

But he replied,

"I will not accept your incense,

I will not accept your rice and salt.

I polish and sell stones for a living,

I am not a sacrificial ritual dancer."


I found a Duoxi① finally,

He accepted my incense,

He accepted my rice,

He accepted my salt.

He said,

"I will worship the lords in heaven,

---

① Duoxi: person who is in charge of reading chants and scriptures to send evil spirits away. They are well-educated people in Yi Group, and also keepers of written and oral literatures.

地神我会祭，
屋里的神我会祭，
屋外的神我会祭。

"要祭房后的山神地神，
要用蜡烛白纸蔬菜来祭它，
要用青树叶来祭它，
要用松枝打卦祭它，
要用母鸡祭它，
要用鸡蛋祭它，
要用老绵羊祭它。
要用母羊和阉羊祭它。"

祭也祭过了，
我爹的病没有好，
我妈的病没有好。
再拿六棵青柏树枝祭它，
拿一棵大竹子祭它，
拿面团祭它，
拿三年的大公鸡祭它，
拿酒饭来祭它。
山神地神祭过了，
我爹的病没有好，
我妈的病没有好。

又祭牲畜神，
牲畜神祭过了，

I will worship the lords on earth,

I will worship the lords in house,

I will worship the lords in field.


"I will worship the Lord of Mountain and Lord of Land,

I will offer up candles, white paper and vegetables,

I will offer up green leaves,

I will offer up pine tree twigs,

I will offer up hens,

I will offer up eggs,

I will offer up old sheep,

I will offer up female sheep and wether."


Although those things were offered up,

My father did not recover,

My mother did not recover.

We offered up six green cypress twigs,

We offered up one big bamboo,

We offered up one flour dough,

We offered up one three-year-old rooster,

We offered up wine and rice.

We worshipped Lord of Mountain and Lord of Land.

My father did not recover,

My mother did not recover.


We worshipped Lord of Livestock.

After all the sacrificial ceremonies,

我爹的病没有好，
我妈的病没有好。

又祭屋里灶君老爷，
灶君老爷祭过了，
我爹的病没有好，
我妈的病没有好。

又祭过往神，
又祭喜丧神，
又祭天上雷神，
又祭河边龙神，
又祭道路神，
祭天神，
祭地神，
又祭七姊妹神，
所有的神都祭过了，
我爹的病没有好，
我妈的病没有好。

又请朵觋来送鬼，
鬼也送过了，
我爹的病没有好，
我妈的病没有好，
爹妈越病越重了！

My father did not recover,

My mother did not recover.


We worshipped Lord of Kitchen.

After all the sacrificial ceremonies,

My father did not recover,

My mother did not recover.


We worshipped Lord of History,

We worshipped Lord of Happy Death①,

We worshipped Lord of Thunder in heaven,

We worshipped Lord of Dragon in river,

We worshipped Lord of Road,

We worshipped the lords in heaven,

We worshipped to the lords on earth,

We worshipped to Lord Seven-sisters.

After all the sacrificial ceremonies,

My father did not recover,

My mother did not recover.


We invited Duoxi to drive the evil spirits away.

After the sacrificial ceremonies,

My father did not recover,

My mother did not recover.

Their illnesses were getting worse.

---

① When some respected aged people, who usually have a happy family, die in their 80s or 90s or even a higher age and in a peaceful way, it is considered as a happy death.

我爹死了，
我妈死了！
我爹死在床头，
我妈死在床尾。
找个聪明人，
去请外家①来。

外家说：
"你爹和你妈，
没有帽子戴，
没有衣裳穿，
没有鞋子穿，
没有银子用。
街头买帽子，
街中买布匹，
街尾买鞋子，
白纸锭像马蹄，
黄纸锭像驴蹄，
样样都要备办齐。"

样样都买来了，
我爹和我妈，
头上戴的有了，
身上穿的有了，

---

① 外家：外祖母家。

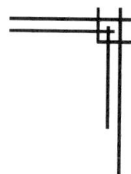

My father died,

My mother died.

My father died on one side of the bed,

My mother died on the other side of the bed.

We sent a wise man,

To invite grandmother's family over.


They came and said,

"Your father and your mother,

They had no hats to wear,

They had no clothes to wear,

They had no shoes to wear,

They had no money to spend.

You need to buy hats for them in the shopping street,

You need to buy clothes for them in the shopping street,

You need to buy shoes for them in the shopping street,

White joss money① is folded into the shape of horse hooves,

Yellow joss money is folded into the shape of donkey hooves,

Everything needs to be prepared properly."


Everything was bought and ready,

My father and mother,

Now there were hats for them to wear,

Now there were clothes for them to wear,

---

① Joss money, also known as the ghost or spirit money, is sheets of paper that are burnt in the traditional Chinese deity and ancestor worship ceremonies. Joss money is also burnt in traditional Chinese funerals.

脚上穿的有了。
挖苦葛藤给爹妈洗脸，
挖苦葛藤给爹妈洗身，
外侄做的麻布包脸嘴，
买来的金头鞋脚上穿，
请人去砍罗汉松，
砍来做棺材。

侄儿侄女来磕头，
大家哭一场。
姑娘送来一只羊，
舅爷送来一只羊，
家里拉出两只羊，
杀了祭我爹，
杀了祭我妈。

棺材停在院里，
棺材头上插花钱，
两口棺材，
像两匹白马。
什么当马鞭？
松树杆当马鞭。
什么当缰绳？
麻索当缰绳。
什么当马掌？
钱纸纸锭当马掌。
两匹白马去到山坡上，
不看松坡不吃草。

Now there were shoes for them to wear.

I washed their faces with roots of the bitter kudzu I dug out,

I washed their bodies with roots of the bitter kudzu I dug out,

I wrapped their faces with the flax cloth made by my nephew,

I put gold shoes I bought on their feet,

I asked people to cut down some Buddhist pines

And to bring wood to make coffins.


Nephews came to mourn,

Families cried together.

One sister sent a sheep,

One uncle sent a sheep,

We took two sheep from home,

And sacrificed them to my father,

And sacrificed them to my mother.


Two coffins were set in the yard,

Joss money was spread on its top,

Two coffins were sitting there

Like two white horses.

What would be taken as a horsewhip?

A pine twig was taken as a horsewhip.

What would be taken as a rein?

A flax rope was taken as a rein.

What would be taken as horseshoes?

Joss money was taken as horseshoes.

The two white horses went to the hill slope,

But not for sightseeing or grass-feeding.

我爹住在石房里，
我妈住在土房里。
我的爹妈啊！
不再在家里住瓦房，
不再在家里睡大床。

让爹住石房，
我心里不愿；
让妈住土房，
我心里不忍！
作揖磕头把他们请回来。

有人劝我说：
"世上鸟兽虫鱼都会死，
皇帝的独儿独女也要死，
有生就有死，
你爹你妈也要死。"

有人劝我说：
"你爹没有死，
你妈没有死，
你爹妈到红杨树林里去了。"

我想爹，
我想妈，
没有父母的儿女，
就像葫芦打水，
一打底就通。

My father would live in a stone house there,

My mother would live in a clay house there.

Oh! My father and mother!

They would not live in our tile-roofed house anymore,

They would not sleep in their big bed in our house anymore.

I felt so reluctant to let my father live in the stone house,

I was unwilling to let my mother live in the clay house.

I kowtowed

Over and over again,

Praying that they would come back.

Someone encouraged me,

"All animals and insects will die,

Even sons and daughters of emperors will die,

Birth is followed by death,

Your father and mother are no exceptions."

Someone encouraged me,

"Your father did not die,

Your mother did not die,

They went into aspen woods."

I missed my father,

I missed my mother,

Men without parents,

Were like gourds

Which were not able to contain water.

没有父母的儿女，
舂面不成团，
舂米不成团。
我要把爹找回来，
我要把妈找回来。

三月十五，
三月二十，
舂好面团团，
舂好米团团，
背起面团团，
背起米团团，
找我爹去，
找我妈去。

找到大河边，
找到刺棵里，
河水哗哗响，
刺棵太戳人。
找到红梨树林里，
找到锥栗树林里，
没有爹的影子，
没有妈的影子。

太阳快落山了，
端起碗吃饭。
吃的什么菜？
吃的河里长的蒿枝菜，

Men without parents,

Were like pounded wheat and rice,

That were not able to be made into dough.

I decided to bring my father back,

I decided to bring my mother back.


On March fifteenth,

On March twentieth,

I made some wheat buns,

And I made some ice balls.

I took the wheat buns,

I took the ice balls,

And I set out to bring my father back,

I set out to bring my mother back.


I went to a big river,

I went through scratchy bushes.

The river water flew roughly,

The bushes were prickly.

I went into red pear woods,

I went into chestnut woods.

I could not find my father anywhere,

I could not find my mother anywhere.


The sun was about to go down,

It was time to take out my meal and eat.

What would I eat?

There was a crown daisy growing in the river,

415

苦得不得了。
带的面团团吃完了，
带的米团团吃完了，
只好转回家，
另外找盘缠。

到了五月间，
小麦割回来，
舂出面团团，
背起面团团，
到处找我爹，
到处找我妈。

找到大河边，
找到荨麻窝，
河水哗哗响，
荨麻辣得很。
找到白杨树林里，
没有爹的影子，
没有妈的影子。
太阳快落山了，
口渴想喝水，
喝的什么水？
喝老树心里的水，
臭得不得了，
带的面团吃完了，
只好转回家，
另外找盘缠。

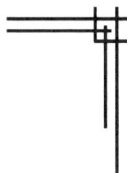

And It tasted so bitter.

The rice balls I took were eaten up,

and the wheat buns I took were eaten up.

I had to go back home,

and tried other ways to finance my next journey.


In the middle of May,

I reaped my wheat,

I made some wheat buns,

I took the wheat buns,

And I set out to look for my father,

I set out to look for my mother.


I went to a big river,

And found a cluster of scratchy nettle plants.

The river water flew roughly,

The nettle plants were stinging.

I went into aspen woods,

I could not find my father anywhere,

And I could not find my mother anywhere.

The sun was about to go down,

I was thirsty and wanted to have something to drink,

What would I drink?

There was some standing water in an old tree trunk,

And it was stinky,

The wheat buns I took were eaten up.

I had to go back home,

and tried other ways to finance my next journey.

到了七月间，
苦荞割回家，
舂成面团团，
背起荞面团，
到处找我爹，
到处找我妈。

找到大河边，
找到刺棵里，
河水哗哗响，
乱刺太戳人。

找到楸木树林里，
找到白木树林里，
没有爹的影子，
没有妈的影子。
太阳落山了，
烧起火堆来过夜，
烧的什么柴？
烧的白樱桃树枝。
烧得火星炸，
睡也睡不着，
眼泪像水流，
鼻涕像蜜淌。
爹妈没找着，
盘缠没有了，
再回家来找盘缠。

In the middle of July,

I reaped my buckwheat,

I made some buckwheat buns,

I took the buckwheat buns,

And I set out to look for my father,

I set out to look for my mother.


I went to a big river,

I went through scratchy bushes.

The river water flew roughly,

The bushes were prickly.


I went into catalpa woods,

I went into whitetree woods,

I could not find my father anywhere,

And I could not find my mother anywhere.

The sun was about to go down,

I set fire to pass the night,

What wood would I burn?

There were some white cherry branches,

The burning branches made crackling sounds.

I could not sleep well,

With my tears shedding like water,

And my nose ran and flowed like honey.

I did not find my parents,

And my money ran out,

　　I had to go back home to find other ways to finance my next

journey.

到了九月间，
下到坝里找包谷，
春成面团团，
背起包谷面团团，
到处找我爹，
到处找我妈。

找到大河边，
遇着放牧人，
问问放牧人，
牧人对我说：
"来帮我放牛，
来帮我放羊，
你爹在什么地方，
我告诉你，
你妈在什么地方，
我告诉你。"

牛羊满山坡，
放到太阳落山了，
放牧人才说：
"我没有看见你爹，
我没有看见你妈，
你要快点走，
怕牛要触你，
怕羊要触你。"

In the middle of September,

I reaped my corn.

I made some corn buns,

I took the corn buns,

And I set out to look for my father,

I set out to look for my mother.


I went to to a big river,

And met a shepherd.

I asked him if he met my parents,

And he said,

"If you help me to herd cattle

And sheep,

I will tell you

Where your father is,

I will tell you,

Where your mother is.

I will tell you."


There were so many cattle and sheep ranging all over the hill

slope,

I herded them until sunset.

But then he said,

"I have never seen your father,

I have never seen your mother,

You need to get out of here quickly,

Otherwise my cattle will attack you,

And my sheep will attack you."

放牛的人哄我，
放羊的人哄我，
放牛的人心不好，
放羊的人心不好。

我找爹妈没找到，
盘缠没有了，
再回家去找盘缠。

到了十月间，
下坝找谷子，
舂成饭团团，
背起饭团团，
到处找我爹，
到处找我妈。

找到石房里，
遇着一位织布老妈妈，
进屋问问老妈妈，
老妈妈忙答话：
"你爹，我晓得，
你妈，我晓得。
你来帮我织麻布，
麻布织好了，
我就说给你。
给你一个麻团团，
麻团前面滚，

The cowherd lied to me,

The shepherd lied to me,

The cowherd was not kind,

The shepherd was not kind.

I did not find my parents,

And my money ran out,

I had to go back home to find other ways to finance my next

journey.

In the middle of October,

I reaped my grain.

I made some rice buns,

I took the rice buns,

And I set out to look for my father,

I set out to look for my mother.

I went to a stone house,

And met a woman who was weaving cloth,

I asked her if she met my parents,

And she answered immediately,

"I know where your father is,

I know where your mother is.

If you help me to weave cloth,

When it is done,

I will tell you.

Here is a ball of flax yarn,

It will roll forward,

你在后面跟。
麻团横处滚，
你往横处找，
麻团滚下坡，
你往坡下找，
麻团滚完了，
你爹找到了，
你妈找到了。"

麻团前面滚，
顺着麻线找，
找到石岩下，
石岩下边江水淌，
麻团滚在江心中，
看爹爹不在，
叫妈妈不应。

江边两岸上，
松树长得直又密，
青冈树长得直又密。
找到松树林里，
找到青冈树林里，
山顶松树像我爹，
山顶青冈树像我妈。
松木砍回来，
青冈木砍回来，
松木刻成爹的像，
青冈木刻成妈的像。

And you will follow the flax yarn.

If the ball rolls across the slope,

You go across the slope.

If the ball rolls downside the slope,

You go across the slope.

When the ball runs out of flax yarn,

You will find your father,

You will find your mother."


The ball of flax yarn rolled forward,

And I followed the flax yarn.

I followed it to a place under a boulder,

Below which there was a river flowing through.

The ball of flax yarn fell into the river and disappeared.

But I did not see my father there,

And I did not see my mother there.


Straight and dense pines

And straight and dense white oaks

Were standing on both sides of the river.

I went into the pine woods,

And I went into the white oak woods.

The pine tree on hilltop looked like my father,

The white oak tree on hilltop looked like my mother.

I cut down the pine tree and took the pine wood back,

I cut down the white oak tree and took the oak wood back.

I carved my father's portrait on the pine wood,

I carved my mother's portrait on the oak wood.

后亲来点眼，
亲戚来点眼，
爹妈的像刻好了，
供在家堂上。
我爹回来了！
我妈回来了！

阿爹啊阿妈！
一月一节令，
每逢节令要祭你。

正月初一来祭你，
二月初八来祭你。
三月二十八，
四月栽种节，
五月端阳节，
六月火把节，
七月十四，
八月中秋，
九月土黄天，

My relatives came to carve the eyes,

and to paint the eyes.

My parents' wood statues were well done,

And I placed them in the central hall.

My father was back.

My mother was back.

Oh! My father and mother!

There is one season in every month,

I will hold a memorial ceremony for you in every season.

I will hold a memorial ceremony for you on January first,

I will hold a memorial ceremony for you on February eighth,

I will hold a memorial ceremony for you on March twenty-eighth,

I will hold a memorial ceremony for you in Planting Festival in April,

I will hold a memorial ceremony for you in Dragon Boat Festival in May,

I will hold a memorial ceremony for you in Torch Festival in June,

I will hold a memorial ceremony for you on July fourteenth,

I will hold a memorial ceremony for you in Mid-autumn Festival Day in August,

I will hold a memorial ceremony for you on the Tuhuang Day① in September,

---

① The literal meaning of Tuhuang Day is yellowish earth day. In Yunnan local culture, it's believed that Tuhuang Day is the sign of the coming of late autumn.

十月初十日，
冬月冬至节，
腊月二十五，
一月一节令，
月月逢节都祭你。

阿爹啊阿妈！
生前你们说：
"人家犁地你就犁，
人家撒种你就撒，
人家放羊你就放。
人家撒种你不撒，
地里就会生野草；
人家放羊你不放，
羊子小得兔儿样。

"房后布谷鸟叫了，
房前李桂秧叫了；
布谷鸟叫就撒种，
李桂秧叫就割荞，
按着节令种庄稼。"

阿爹啊阿妈！
照着你们说的做，
五谷丰收，
人畜两旺。

I will hold a memorial ceremony for you on October tenth,

I will hold a memorial ceremony for you on day of Winter Solstice in November,

I will hold a memorial ceremony for you on December twenty-fifth.

There is one season in every month,

I will hold a memorial ceremony for you in every season.


Oh! My father and mother!

You often told me,

"Go plow the fields when others are doing so,

Go sow seeds when others are doing so,

Go herd the the sheep when others are doing so.

If you do not sow when others do,

Weed will grow in your fields.

If you do not herd when others do,

Sheep will grow no larger than little rabbits.


"When cuckoo birds are singing behind our house,

It is time to go sow seeds.

When Liguiyang are singing in front of our house,

It is time to go reap buckwheat.

Grow crops in accordance with the laws of seasonal arrangements."


Oh! My father and mother!

I will follow your advice and do what you told me to.

Our crops will grow well and strong and there will always be good harvests,

Our livestock will be flourishing and our whole family will be prosperous.